WHERE GHOSTS WALK

Where Ghosts Walk

The Haunts of Familiar Characters in History and Literature

By

Marion Harland

Author of " Some Colonial Homesteads," etc.

Illustrated

Fourth Impression

G. P. PUTNAM'S SONS
NEW YORK AND LONDON
The Knickerbocker Press
1913

The Knickerbocker Press, New York

To My Daughters,—

CHRISTINE TERHUNE HERRICK,

IN WHOSE DEAR COMPANY I VISITED THE SCENES SKETCHED
IN THESE PAGES,

AND

VIRGINIA BELLE VAN DE WATER,

MY PATIENT AND FAITHFUL AMANUENSIS IN THE
PREPARATION OF THE MANUSCRIPT
FOR THE PRESS,—

THIS VOLUME IS
AFFECTIONATELY DEDICATED.

MARION HARLAND.

London, England,
August, 1898.

Five of the sketches included in this book are reprinted by the courtesy of the publishers, Harper & Brothers, from the columns of *Harper's Bazar*.

CONTENTS

ILLUSTRATIONS

* By permission of Mr. Charles Moore.

Illustrations xi

I

TWO LITTLE ROOMS

I

TWO LITTLE ROOMS

THE " Supping-Room " of Mary Stuart, in Holyrood Palace, is the smallest of the royal suite. It is a mere closet, and now bare and depressing to a degree utterly incompatible with our ideas of tolerable comfort, until we remind ourselves that the stone walls were once masked by richly wrought hangings and the cold floors softened by carpets brought, or imported, by Mary into rugged Scotland from her beloved France.

A small door opens into a closet used for storing wines and other accompaniments of the *petits soupers* which the Queen was fond of giving to her intimates. The entrance to the supping-room is from her bedchamber. The walls of this are still hung with tapestries selected

3

by her, a faded confusion of knights in armour and plunging horses. The canopied bed, covered with a tattered silk coverlet, was also hers. Over the mantel is a half-length portrait of Queen Elizabeth. We hope—mercifully—that it was not here in her hapless rival's time.

The tapestry is looped away from the door of the supping-room, and from another and a smaller door close beside it, raised by a single step from the floor. This leads to the winding stone stair connecting the Queen's bedchamber with Darnley's. The little door is kept locked. Darnley had the key, and his alone was the right to use it on Saturday night, the ninth of March, 1566, when Queen Mary had bidden a few friends to supper. How few, we comprehend as we survey the tiny withdrawing-room. Her half-sister, the Countess of Argyle, two ladies-in-waiting, a couple of gentlemen of the Court, a page who held the candles, and her Italian Secretary, David Rizzio, must have crowded the closet to discomfort when the table and chairs were in place.

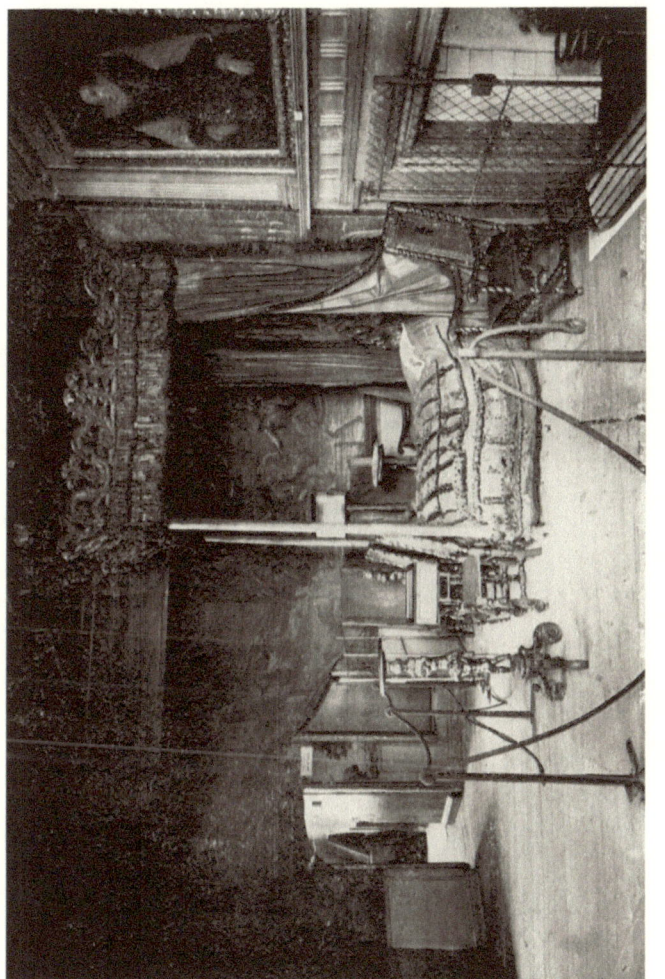

QUEEN MARY'S BEDROOM, HOLYROOD PALACE.

When Darnley—otherwise King Henry and husband of the Queen, who, like Saul, was higher than any of the people from his shoulders and upward,—stooped to clear the lintel of the low doorway, and showed to the party his handsome face, flushed with wine, nobody was surprised. As he seated himself upon the elbow of his wife's chair, and put his arm about her waist, the fairest face in all Scotland was lifted, smilingly expectant, to his. The change of position showed to Mary what she, at the first glance, mistook for the ghost of Lord Ruthven, in full armour, filling up the door behind her. He had arisen from a sick-bed to lead the conspirators.

We all know the story,—better perhaps than any other in the records of a land whose history is a continuous romance. Rizzio, torn from his frantic clinging to the skirts of his Royal employer, was dragged through the bedroom and through the larger audience-room beyond, there dispatched by fifty-six dagger-thrusts, then kicked, like a dead dog,

down the palace stairs into the court
below.

In an affidavit prepared by Ruthven he
"takes God to record that the said Davie
received never a stroke in Her Majesty's
presence, nor was not stricken till he was
at the farthest door of Her Majesty's utter
chamber."

His insistence upon this evidence of
respectful forbearance in the Royal
presence may be a cruel refinement of
punctilio, but, if it be true, it disposes
thoroughly of the historic blood-stains
upon the floor of the little inner room,
which even Sir Walter Scott was disposed
to believe genuine, and which the con-
scientious annalist, Robert Chambers, does
not gainsay. We look vainly for them
to-day and openly avow our disappointment. The hoary custodian declares
boldly that he "got tired of renewing"
the brown blotches.

"The floor was relaid two hundred and
more years ago," he says. "Yet I found
the stains here when I came, and when
they wore out visitors insisted upon seeing

them. So "—with a shrug that is more
French than Scottish—"what was I to
do ?"

The first shock of disillusionment over,
imagination rallies to contemplate the
actual features of the tragedy. Queries
which no man living can answer, and
touching which contemporary records are
mute, press to our lips.

Did Mary sleep in her own bed that
night? Was the Sunday-morning interview with her weak and vicious boy-hus-
band that terminated in their reconciliation,
held in the bedroom, or in the audience-
chamber beyond ? By what wiles did he
induce her to forego the purpose expressed in the impassioned outbreak that
met his first words of penitence ?

" You have done me such a wrong that
neither the recollection of our early friendship, nor all the hope you can give me of
the future, can ever make me forget it ! "

Darnley " thankfully received " her half-
brother Murray on Sabbath evening, and
Mary would not suffer her kinsman to
sup with Morton as had been planned,

but kept him with her all the evening.
She "embraced and kissed him, alleging
that in case he had been at home, he
would not have suffered her to have been
so incourteously handled."

Did the three, Darnley, Murray, and
Murray's sister, whose talk "so moved
him that the tears fell from his eyne," sup
amicably and not uncheerfully in this room
that Sunday night?

On Monday, "Her Majesty took the
King by one hand and the Earl of Murray by the other, and walked in her utter
chamber "—*i. e.*, the audience-chamber upon the threshold of which Rizzio's blood
was hardly dry—"the space of an hour."

What did they talk of while pacing the
floor over which the shrieking favourite
was dragged by his murderers forty-eight
hours before?

History never has, and never will clear
up the "muddle."

Her child—James First of England
and Sixth of Scotland—was born on the
nineteenth of June of that same year, in
another little room no larger than the

supping-closet of Holyrood, but in the
stronger Castle of Edinburgh.   The walls
are panelled with oak, blackened by age.
The initials " M. R." and " I. R." are
wrought into the carvings of the ceiling.
A shield upon the wall above the fireplace
bears the inscription :

"19 JVNII. 1566."

Above the only spot in the room where
the bed could have stood, the royal arms
are emblazoned, and beneath is what pur-
ports to be " the young mother's prayer
of thanksgiving on that auspicious occasion "—in black-letter :

Lord Jesu Chryst, that crownit was with Thorne,
Preserve the Birth, quhais Badgie heir is borne,
And send Hir Sonne successione, to Reigne still
Lang in this Realme, if that it be thy will.
Als grant, O Lord, quhat ever of Hir proceed,
Be to thy Glorie, Honer and Prais, sobied.

The spacious apartment adjoining the
wee inner room was tapestried for Mary's
use with " cloth-of-gold and brocaded taf-
feta.   The floors were covered with Turk-
ish rugs, the tables were of massive oak,

elaborately carved; the chairs were covered with gilded leather and had cushions
of brocade and damask."

We hearken indifferently to the catalogue, and turn back to our little room.
Mary entered Edinburgh Castle, by the
advice of her Privy Council, on the third
of April, and, as was the royal etiquette in
such circumstances, took to her chamber
on the third of June. From the single
window of this she looked down upon her
capital city, that had already begun to dis-
trust her. Beyond the housetops towered
the broad bulk of Arthur's Seat, seen at a
greater distance than from Holyrood, but
in the perspective looking yet more like a
couchant lion, watchful of Scotland's honour and Scotland's religion. She must almost have hated the sight of it during
that weary fortnight of waiting.

The room is irregular in shape and less
than eight feet square. The bed must
have been a mere cot, and if other besides
Mary Beaton—now Lady Boyne—and
the court physician were present, there
could not have been left space for more

HOLYROOD PALACE, WITH ARTHUR'S SEAT IN THE DISTANCE.

furniture than the quaint arm-chair still standing against the wainscot and which we are told was here then.

Yet tall Darnley was accompanied by at least one friend when he visited his wife at two o'clock of the same day, the Prince having been born between nine and ten in the morning. Mary, with her own hand, drew aside the coverings from the baby's face.

"My Lord," she said, solemnly, "GOD has given us a son."

She would have been more than woman if, in the weakness of the hour, she had not referred to the risk she and the heir to the crown had run on that awful Saturday night, three months agone.

"Sweet Madam," pleaded the father (himself not yet one-and-twenty), "is this the promise that you made, that you would forget and forgive all?"

"I have forgiven all," said the Queen. "I never will forget."

Darnley fidgeted uneasily.

"Madam, these things are past."

"Then," was the answer, "let them go."

The record of this interview is the only glimpse we have of anything that passed in the strait birth-chamber in the after part of that day.

Before the visitor enters the Castle his attention is directed to a section of comparatively new masonry in the outer wall in ominous juxtaposition to the board lettered, "QUEEN MARY'S APARTMENTS." The story told and believed by guides and townspeople, and set down without comment in guide-books to Edinburgh Castle, is that, in 1830, workmen engaged in repointing the masonry noticed that the wall sounded hollow at that spot, and removed several stones to get at the cavity. They found behind them in "a recess measuring about two feet six inches by one foot," the skeleton of a male infant in an oak coffin, "evidently of great antiquity and much decayed."

I copy the rest of the record :

"The remains were wrapped in a cloth, believed to be woollen, very thick, and somewhat resembling leather, and within this the remains of a richly embroidered

silk covering.   Two initials were wrought
upon it, and one of them, an *I*, was dis-
tinctly visible.   By order of Major-General
Thackery, then commanding the Royal
Engineers, the crumbling relic of humanity
was again restored to its peculiar resting-
place, and the aperture closed up."

We discuss, in guarded tones, the
incident that may have been an Event,
while we stand in the deeply embrasured
window of the little room, the black-letter
inscription, which Mary did *not* indite,
before us.   Then we pass, treading lightly,
as might befit the bearers of a moment-
ous state secret, into the larger apartment
for a critical inspection of the unpleasing
visage of James First of England and
Sixth of Scotland.   "The son who, I
hope, shall first unite the two kingdoms
of Scotland and England," said Mary to
an English gentleman who accompanied
Darnley upon the visit alluded to just
now.

The peace of both kingdoms and the
perpetuity of Scottish national existence
depended upon the breath of the infant

whose birth was preceded by such stress of battle, murder, and sudden death as might well have cost mother and child their lives.

His father, near akin to both Mary and Elizabeth, was "a comely Prince, of a fair and large stature of body, pleasant in countenance, affable to all men, as well exercised in martial pastimes upon horse-back as any Prince of that age, but was so facile he could conceal no secret," writes one historian.   Another—" He was of a comely stature, and none was like unto him within this island . . . prompt and ready for all games and sports." Still another, that he was "accomplished in all excellent endowments, both of body and of mind."

The personal and mental charms of Mary Stuart need no recapitulation.   No other woman known to history, Cleopatra not excepted, ever exercised such magic sway over whomsoever she willed to captivate.

Her best authenticated portrait, taken when she was Dauphine of France, is

upon the same wall and in a line with
that of " James VI., son of Queen Mary
and Lord Henry Darnley."

We look from the pictured face of the
beautiful woman to that of the homely,
boorish successor of two famous queens,
recalling that he was also gawky in carriage, plebeian in taste, and so cowardly
that he padded his doublet for fear of
the assassin's knife, and loathed the sight
of warlike weapons,—and account this,
the offspring of royal parents, a freak of
heredity. With a sort of passionate curiosity that burns within us like a fever,
we query again, and always vainly, what
never-to-be-revealed scenes went on in
that little room on the nineteenth day of
June, 1566, where lately wedded Mary
Beaton kept guard over the exhausted
mother and the Prince who was to unite
the kingdoms of Scotland and of England.

II

"ONLY A BUT AN' A BEN"

II

"ONLY A BUT AN' A BEN"

TO say that the "auld clay biggin" in which Robert Burns was born is humble and homely, even for a peasant's thatched cottage, is to give an inadequate idea of the place to one who has never stood within it. The four-roomed story-and-a-half Shakespeare house at Stratford-on-Avon is commodious and more than respectable beside it.

If chimney, dresser, pantry, and bed-place were taken out of the "but," or kitchen, we should have a chamber measuring fifteen feet one way and sixteen the other. The projections I have enumerated contract the clear space to about ten feet. The floor is of flat stones, irregularly laid, and the interstices are filled with mortar. The "bed-place" is a niche in the wall opposite the chimney—a common feature in Scottish farmsteads and cottages. It is between three and four feet deep, and a trifle over five feet long, and is filled by a bed covered with a dark counterpane of homespun. The open front is protected by a coarse network of wire, as royal regalia and delicate works of art are shielded from lawless handling. Blue curtains, that, when closed, hid bed and occupants, are pulled back to reveal recess and furniture. Bedstead there is none, the bedding being laid upon a ledge of like material with the stone and plaster walls. A valance hangs from it to the floor.

The alcove is a darksome hole, even now that modern prejudice has cut a window of fair size in the front wall of the lowly room. All the daylight that made its way to the eyes of the new-born baby boy, one hundred and thirty-nine years agone, stole in through an opening eighteen inches deep, filled with four six-inch

"BED-PLACE" IN WHICH BURNS WAS BORN.

panes of glass, set in a heavy sash. This
window looks out upon a grass-plot that
then formed a part of the "sma' croft"
tilled by "William Burns, Farmer," as he
is described upon the family grave in Al-
loway Kirkyard.

We gasp involuntarily as the civil custodian tells the story of the solitary window, and points out that there was no
outer door to the "but."

Her consolatory remark, "There was
the light from the fireplace, of course,"
helps us to reconstruct for ourselves a
scene with which she and other "improvements" have nothing to do.

The faint blue reek pervading the room
from the low peat fire in the grate gives a
touch of local atmosphere essentially Scottish. The fire burned more brightly on
that stormy January night of 1759. We
close our eyes and see the mother, weak
and thankful, in the shadowy recess, the
group of kindly gossips bustling about
her and the new-comer, and the proud
father receiving the congratulations of the
gypsy tramp, who predicted:

" He 'll hae misfortunes great an' sma',
    But ay a heart aboon them a',
    He 'll be a credit to us a',
       We 'll a' be proud o' Robin."

The deal dresser filled up, as now, all the back of the room not occupied by window and bed-place. In the middle of the floor was the table at which, we are told, the father sat to read Shakespeare to his family on winter nights, and about which the household gathered for meals and evening prayers. It is pushed against the dresser to leave space for the passage of tourist visitors. This oblong product of country carpentry is scarred all over with the names of those whose signatures,

    " Like their faces,
Do much abound in public places "

that are consecrated ground to angels and right-minded men. At the corner of the ingle was the old spinning-wheel, now to be seen in the other room, where it probably stood, still and silent, on the birthnight. Elbow-room must have been as rare a luxury as sofa and carpet in the "but" (which was kitchen, bedroom, sitting-room, and bedchamber all in one), when the children's stools, the table, wheel, and the parents' chairs were in place. One of the latter, bound over and about with cords, lest it should be sat upon, backs up against the "set-in" bed.

One rapid sweep of fancy collects the household, as in " The Cotter's Saturday Night," a faithful portraiture of Burns's own home-life. We group the elder bairns and the "wee things," the "lisping infant prattling on the father's knee," the busy mother who

> " Wi' her needle an' her shears,
> Gars auld claes look amaist as weel 's new,"

"the eldest hope, their Jenny, woman grown," not forgetting the "strappan youth," her lover—and wonder unto despair how furniture and people got into the room ; how the home party ate their supper of "halesome parritch," milk, oatcake, and cheese, then knelt about the "saint, the father and the husband," while he prayed.

"Where did the children sleep?" is our natural query.

"This was the only bedroom. The parlor was seldom used except upon grand occasions, such as christenings, marriages, funerals, and the like."

We listen and disbelieve. The civil custodian was no more here on that January night than we were. We insist mentally and stubbornly upon transferring the elder bairns, the wee toddlers, and lisping infant, for the nonce, to the "ben," or parlor. "A but an' a ben" was the conventional thing in cottage architecture at that date. This particular "ben" is an uninteresting room, notwithstanding our arbitrary plenishings of cots and pallets for the "hantle" of juvenile Burnses. It is separated from the "but" by a small hall, about five feet square. Into this the front door, set in the exact middle of the house, opens. It is double-leaved, and a wrought-iron hook, eighteen inches long, made fast to the wall, when hasped, kept one half of it shut, leaving the other free for the coming and going of family and friends. The house is flush with the village street, and was formerly secured against intruders by a latch, above which a bit of wood was stuck at night so it could not be lifted from without.

Like the "but," the "ben" had but one window at the date of the overflow of younglings which we have decided was imperatively necessary on that stormy birthnight. This one inlet of air and light was in the streetward wall, and had six panes, six inches long by four wide, in each sash.

Yet the room was airy and cheerful by comparison with the more important "but." The practical, humane sisterhousewife cannot but hope that when

"November chill blew loud wi' angry sigh,"

the "thrifty wife" so far defied the Ayrshire Grundy as to take her needle, shears, and making-over to this larger room to spare her eyesight.

A round light-stand that belonged to the Burnses is here, and half of one wall

is covered by an old sign-board, defaced
by initial-cutting. A portrait of Burns,
rudely painted, and much the worse for
weather, adorns the board, which hung in
front of the cottage after it passed out of
the elder Burns's hands and became a
public-house. It was purchased by the
trustees of the Burns Monument several
years ago, and is kept in excellent repair.
The brown thatch of the roof is a foot
and a half thick, and beautifully laid and
trimmed.

The addition of two other rooms for
the storage of relics is in exact keeping
with the original building. Two chairs
from the Ayr public-house, lettered " Tam
o' Shanter" and " Souter Johnny," a tod-
dy-ladle used by Burns in Nance Tinnock's
house, a deal " leaf-table," and a brass
candlestick, once his property, are passed
hastily by as we catch a glimpse of a book
of his autograph letters and the original
manuscript of " Tam o' Shanter." Burns
wrote a strong, legible hand, not in the
least like the sprawling characters of the
average self-taught man. Two of the

THE BURNS COTTAGE.

"The auld clay biggin'."

best-known lines of the famous poem are
usually printed and quoted thus :

> " Or, like the snow-fall on the river,
>   One moment white, then gone forever."

An unexpurgated and careful Edinburgh edition has them,—

> " Or, like the snow-falls on the river,
>   One moment white—then melts forever."

The peasant poet boldly uses "like"
as a synonym for "as "—a common pro-
vincialism in our Southern States and in
some parts of England at this day :

> " Or, like the snow falls in the river,
>   One moment white—then melts forever."

The compound word " snow-falls " is a
modern alteration that improves neither
figure nor syntax.

" Only a but an' a ben !" We say it
musingly, leaning over the railing on the
top of the inharmonious Grecian temple
erected to the memory of the ploughman
genius.

The lovely visible pastoral spread below
us, and as far as the eye can reach, is all

"the Burns country." Thus it is set
down in guide-books; thus the passionate
pilgrim from the Land of the Sunset
names it in exulting tenderness. These
are Robert Burns's hills, green to the
brows, and dotted with trees. The low-
lands, where cattle feed and men are
ploughing, and driving home loaded wains
to the rickyard, include the fields hal-
lowed by his toil. His ploughshare up-
rooted the daisy, and it was no longer a
weed; in unearthing a field-mouse it
made the "wee, sleekit, cow'rin', tim'rous
beastie" pathetic and symbolic for all
time. The smell of peat in the sun-filled
air is as sweet to us for his sake as the
perfume of the hardy late roses growing
about the base of his monument; the ripple of the Doon filling up the silences
of the dreamy day is set to the music of
his verse.

His spirit does not haunt—it *possesses*
our willing souls in bonny, bonny Ayrshire.

Yet—only "a but an' a ben!"

III

"HER GLOOMY HONEYMOON"

III

"HER GLOOMY HONEYMOON"

IN the great Babylon of Hampton Court
Palace, builded by Thomas Wolsey—
butcher-boy, Cardinal, Premier, ruined and
disgraced favourite—there remains but one
authentic portrait of him. That one is a
quarter-length cabinet picture in an ill-
lighted closet, called by his name.

Henry the Eighth robbed his arrogant
vizier of his palace and altered it to suit
his own taste. The groined ceiling of
"Anne Boleyn's Gateway" is decorated
with true-lovers' knots binding together
the initials " H " and " A." The magnificent Great Hall was begun at the same
time.

" By dint of ye men workyng in theyr
houre tymes and drynking tymes for the
hastye expedicion of ye same, and ye emp-

cion of tallow candles spent by ye workmen in ye nyght-tymes," carvings, and illuminated panels all ablaze with gold-leaf and carmine, and matchless tapestries, brought from the uttermost parts of the earth, that even now glow with fadeless colours, were finished before Jane Seymour's death at Hampton Court. Her initials are intertwined with Henry's among the ornaments of the ceiling, and in mosaics at the door of the chapel in which he afterward married Katharine Howard.

The large picture catalogued as " Henry VIII. and his Family," that hangs in the Queen's Audience-Chamber, was painted by an artist of the Holbein school. The King and his little son, who became Edward VI., occupy the centre of the picture. Jane Seymour, who died at her boy's birth, nevertheless appears seated at Henry's left hand. Next to this posthumous portrait stands the Princess Elizabeth. Opposite to her, and at the King's right, is the Princess Mary.

We look vainly among the hundreds of portraits in the immense collection of the

WOLSEY'S HALL, HAMPTON COURT.

Royal Palace for any other likeness of
Mary Tudor, first Queen-regnant of England and Ireland, who became, in the
fulness of time, the most sorrowful and
most unpopular sovereign who ever sat
upon the English throne. For the first
eleven years of her life she was the pre-
cocious and petted darling of parents and
people. After that, her story is made up
of variations of tragedy. Her father declared her illegitimate and sought her life ;
her idolised mother died, begging, with
futile tears, for a last glimpse of her only
child ; Anne Boleyn's flouts and insults to
her worse than orphaned step-daughter
were like a weight about the step-mother's
neck when she came to the scaffold ; the
girl's dearest in heart and next of kin died
by the hand of the executioner for no
crime save their love and loyalty to her.
Her wild and lasting grief for her mother's
death undermined her health hopelessly.
She never knew another well day. Before
she came into the kingdom so hardly secured for herself and her adherents, Mary
Tudor had known outrages that might well

3

convert the saint she seemed to those who knew her as Princess, into the incarnate devil she is held to have been by the Protestant world.

But to our portrait. It was painted when she was about twenty-eight years of age, and more than pleasing in appearance. At eighteen, she was reckoned a beauty. At thirty-eight, the Venetian ambassador at her court wrote :

" Her face is well-formed, and her features prove that when younger she was more than moderately handsome. She would now be so, saving some wrinkles, caused more by sorrow than by age."

The pictured eyes into which we are now looking are dark and lustrous ; her complexion is pale, but pure. One writer says it was " singularly beautiful. Until the latest years of her heavily shadowed life her blush was as quick and vivid as a girl's."

In 1554, being then in the fortieth year of her age, " she kept her gloomy honeymoon at Hampton Court Palace," records a biographer. The Duke of Norfolk, her

HAMPTON COURT PALACE.

staunch old friend and ally, "whom the Queen loved entirely," died when she had been married but a few days.   The Court went into mourning, and Mary, we may well believe, not unwillingly, withdrew with her young husband, Don Philip of Spain, to the superb abode begun by Wolsey and completed by her father.   There is no finer palace in all Great Britain.   When Mary, whose favourite seat it was, entered it with such of her bridal train as she chose to bring with her, it was like a dream of Eastern magnificence.

A glance from the picture to the great windows on the other side of the room reveals gardens, avenues, and terraces that then stretched away as far as the eye could reach in every direction, except where they were bounded by the silvery Thames. Mary was a loving and a skilful horti-culturist, and never happier than when engaged among her flowers and orchards. Music was a passion with her from in-fancy, and she was no mean performer upon "the virginals" and the harpsichord. She was an accomplished scholar, and had

in her girlhood pleased her fourth step-
mother, Katharine Parr, by translating the
Gospel of St. John from the Latin into English.   Books, music, and such treasures of
art as were collected under no other roof in
all her kingdom, were here, subject to her
demand.   The bridegroom, whom she had
" received right lovingly " upon his arrival
in England, had already established that
fell influence over her which was to prove
alike inexplicable to her apologists and to
her accusers.

A portrait of Philip of Spain in this same
Hampton Court gallery partially justifies
the infatuation of the bride, who was eleven
years his senior.   It shows us a martial figure, a commanding presence, and a noble,
open countenance.   If it were indeed taken
for him, it was egregiously flattered.   Con-
temporaries and other portraits concur in
asserting that he was forbidding in face
and churlish in manner.   " His complexion was cane-coloured, his hair sandy and
scanty, his eyes small, blue, and weak, with
a gloomy expression of countenance,"—
we hear from one.   From another that he

was " a man of mean presence and carroty
complexion."   The English people had
dreaded his alliance with their Queen with
aversion that seems to us like a premonition of the woes it would bring upon them.
Instead of seeking to conciliate them, as
Mary implored him to do, he ran counter
to their prejudices from the outset.   While
they sympathised with the Queen in her
grief for her friend's death, they divined
shrewdly that her rigid retirement was
Philip's work, not hers, and were highly
incensed thereat.

" Since the Spanish wedlock, Hampton
Court gates that used to be open all day
long are closed, and every man must give
an account of his errand before entering,"
is a complaint made during the gloomy
honeymoon.

Curiously enough, the only glimpse we
have at what went on within the locked
gates, is in the shape of a fast-day bill-of-
fare, in which salt fish, fresh sturgeon
caught in the Thames, crabs, and eels, are
succeeded by apples, oatmeal, and cream,
and these by cheese, wafers, and fruit as a

dessert. One might fancy that bride and groom were preparing themselves by fasting and prayer for the crusade of blood and fire inaugurated by Spanish rule. The stipulation in the marriage contract that Philip should " aid the Queen in governing her kingdoms," had been followed up by instructions to her privy councillor, written by her own hand, to " tell the King the whole state of the realm, and to obey his commandment in all things."

Behind, and at the right of the gentle-faced Princess in the picture before us, is the uncouth figure of " Jane the Fool," who had been attached to Mary's person and followed her journeyings for years, as privileged jester and chamberwoman. Jane married a servant in the household of the Princess Elizabeth before Mary's coronation and marriage. Had she been in attendance during the Hampton Court seclusion, she might have told her royal mistress some stinging and salutary truths ; even proposed, after the manner of kings' jesters, to exchange titles with her.

With all the acres of tapestries and paint-

ings within-doors, and the enchanting miles
of woods and water and pleasure-grounds
without, in which he might roam unseen
and undisturbed, Philip was desperately
ennuyé before the gloomy honeymoon was
over.   On the other hand, his mature bride,
so long and so sadly lonely in heart, became the more madly enamoured of the
only being she had had the right to claim
as her own since her mother died.

The best authorities upon historical
dates now agree that the reconciliation of
the estranged sisters, Mary and Elizabeth,
took place in the second month of Mary's
nominal mourning for Norfolk and real en-
joyment of the society of her ungracious
husband.   The meeting was in Mary's
bedchamber.   A stormy dialogue con-
cluded with a kiss and the gift from the
Queen of a costly ring.   Gossiping tradition will have it that Philip wrought upon
his wife to recall her sister, and that he
was concealed, with Mary's knowledge,
behind the arras during the interview, that
she might be strictly obedient to his instructions.

We find the Queen again at Hampton
Court in April, 1555, when "the King's
Grace"—he was *that* to the terrified na-
tion from the hour he emerged from the
gloomy seclusion of his honeymoon—"removed the Queen to Hampton Court to
keep Easter and to take her chamber
there." The phrase had reference to the
Court etiquette that required the sovereign to keep her room for a month before the birth of a child.

Tennyson puts a *Magnificat* into Mary's
mouth with the beginning of the illusive
hope to which she was to cling until her
forlorn case became the laughing-stock of
the nations.

" O Philip, husband ! now thy love to mine
   Will cling more close, and these bleak manners
      thaw,
   That make me shamed and tongue-tied in my
      love !—"

is an apostrophe that is hardly a poetical
licence.

Her long silence and absence from
public life were at length explained by a

despatch to the French King from a plain-spoken ambassador :

"The Queen's state is by no means of the hopeful kind generally supposed, but rather some woful malady, for she sits whole days on the ground, crouched together, with her knees higher than her head."

Fox corroborates this in his history of the martyrs of this blood-soaked reign :

"Sometimes she laid weeks without speaking, as one dead, and more than once the rumour went that she *had* died."

Another pitying chronicler alludes to her as "the half-dead Queen," while depicting the horrible cruelties perpetrated by Philip and his lieutenant, Gardiner, before the breath at last forsook her dropsical body.

In 1557, Philip returned from a long visit to Spain to fan the sinking flames of persecution and to drag the invalid from her bed into the light as evidence that he had her warrant for all that he did.   His object gained, he sailed again for his native land, leaving her to bear the onus of his deeds.

It was after this second departure that, convinced that he had deserted her, the tormented creature, old before her time, despised as well as abandoned, in a paroxysm of despair, cut his portrait from the frame and trampled it under her feet.

She was brought upon a litter to Hampton Court—"the which she ever loved the most of all her abodes"—in September, 1558, "but grew the worse, rather than better," as was to be expected,—haunted as palace and gardens must have been by ghosts from the irrevocable Past.

She died in St. James's Palace, November 17th of the same year. "It was the custom for the body of an English sovereign to be buried in royal array, but Mary had earnestly entreated that no semblance of the crown which had pressed so heavily on her brow in life might cumber her corpse in death. She requested that she might be interred as a poor *religieuse*."

It is hard to breathe in all the glory and spaciousness of the state rooms, while we review the dreary, dreary tale. At the upper end of the Great Hall, where Henry VIII. danced with Jane Seymour and Katharine Howard, and where Katharine Parr was proclaimed Queen, is a dais or platform, upon which Shakespeare and his company played in Elizabeth's time. Other and less august shades people it for us as we stroll pensively from one tapestried wall to the other, and picture to ourselves how the Hall must look when closed for the night and but faintly illuminated by the moonbeams struggling through the stained glass of the tall windows. An archway opening from the great staircase to the Queen's apartments, in what a historian calls "the mysterious angle of Hampton Court," was built up two centuries and more ago, for no other reason, said superstitious gossips, than to impede the wanderings of Jane Seymour, who used to roam the galleries and flit up and down the staircase, a lighted candle in her hand. We have been told, to-day, in our round of the palace, that she has been seen here within a dozen years. Katharine Howard, when arrested in her

own apartments at Hampton Court, and
told that she was to be taken to the Tower,
ran shrieking through the corridors, hair
dishevelled and dress disordered, to the
closed door of the chapel, where she knew
Henry was then praying, and beat upon
the panels with her hands, calling wildly
upon her husband's name. She was torn
away, and borne to her death,—"albeit
she struggled violently, and her screams
were heard by everyone in the chapel."
Since which time she has haunted the
corridor—a distraught phantom with
streaming hair, who cries frantically to
her royal lord for pardon and help. The
nurse of Edward VI. turns an invisible
spinning-wheel and mutters to herself in
the room once occupied by her.

If foul wrongs done to a woman while
she lived, and merciless judgment meted
out to her when dead, could recall the departed, Great Hall and bedchamber and
closet would be revisited daily and nightly
by the sad wraith of her whose brief reign
is like the stamp of a bloody hand upon
the page of English history bearing date

of 1553-1558.   Calm   reason   may   not
plead for Mary Tudor, but our hearts are
sore with pity as we make hers the central
figure upon our stage ; first, as the sweet-
faced translator of the Evangel of Love,
petite in form, exquisite in complexion,
"both wise and sage, and beautiful in
favour" ; then, the slighted wife, bereft
alike of the dream of motherhood and a
husband's love,—finally, broken in spirit
and in health, "hated by her husband as
hated by her people" ; grovelling, like a
dying animal, upon the ground for days
together, dumbly awaiting welcome death
in the lordly rooms where she had spent
her prophetic honeymoon.

IV

"AN EATING-HOUSE FOR GOODLY FARE"

IV

"AN EATING-HOUSE FOR
GOODLY FARE"

" JUST as it was two hundred years
ago, do you say?"

"It was old in 1725. A handbook of
London published at that date catalogues
it as *Ye Olde Cheshire Cheese Tavern, near
ye Flete Prison, an Eating-House for goodly
fare.* You see it now just as it was then.
That is Dr. Samuel Johnson's corner over
there. Goldsmith sat at his left hand.
Goldsmith's lodgings were just across the
street. He wrote the *Vicar of Wakefield*
in them. I 'll show you his grave in the
Temple Churchyard, when we go out.
That is, unless I can persuade you to stay
here to luncheon. It will be something to
remember, I assure you."

The intonation is persuasive and a little

anxious.   The speaker casts a deprecating
smile at the trio of fashionably attired
women he is escorting.   The one directly
addressed gathers up her black satin skirt
from the sawdusty floor, includes the ap-
pointments and inmates of the room in
one sweeping, shuddering glance, and says
hastily,—" O *no !* thank you *ever* so much,
but I really could n't *think* of it ! "

Nobody, excepting ourselves, looks at
the party that has the effect of taking up
all the spare room in the place, and making the ceiling lower, the wainscoted walls
more dingy, in a way peculiar to over-
dressed Americans.   The *cicerone* is their
countryman, but of a different stamp.
There is intelligent regret in his backward
glance as he follows the disdainful bevy
in their retreat.   We get a glimpse of
them through a window, when they emerge
from the shabby doorway.   They are still
gathering their skirts about them, and pick
their way gingerly upon their boot-tips
over the wet stones of Wine Court.

So far as we can see, the flutter and
bustle produced by their hurried round of

ENTRANCE TO THE "OLD CHESHIRE CHEESE" IN WINE OFFICE COURT.

From an Original Drawing by Herbert Railton.

inspection is confined to ourselves, although every word uttered was audible
from wall to wall. The ruffled stillness
subsides with their departure, as stagnant
waters regain placidity after the plashing
of a stone. We exchange congratulatory
smiles and snuggle down contentedly in
our nook across the aisle from the John-
sonian corner. Then, the encompassing
atmosphere begins to take effect. We
grow dreamily reminiscent, patiently an-
ticipative.

This expedition to the one coffee-
house in London that has withstood the
surge of "modern improvements" directed against building and management for
more than two hundred years, is the
"larkiest" thing we have done in our
wanderings. Before coming, it looked to
us like a bit of Bohemian adventure verg-
ing upon the poisonous sweetness of stolen
waters, the touch of iniquity which, the
witty Frenchwoman said, was all that was
needed to make her vanilla ice perfectly
delicious. We foresaw a fair measure of
novel excitement, with a certain back-

ground of discomfort. As the spirit of
the place and the times gains possession
of us, the "lark" becomes more than decorous.   It is dignified, and a duty we owe
to the *manes* of the greater than ourselves
who resorted hither in the dim and reverend Past.

The coffee-house — or chop-house — is
smaller than we expected to find it. There
is a bar on the other side of the hall, with
a sustained reputation of its very own,
and the supper-rooms above-stairs could
tell gay tales of dead-and-gone revelries,
if the dumb walls were phonographic.
This, the chief resort of customers that
have given " The Cheshire Cheese " world-
wide renown, is not more than twenty feet
long and perhaps fifteen feet in width.
There are ten tables, each with seats for
six upon hard benches that are made fast
to the floor. Breast-high partitions between the tables make compartments like
the square family pews seen in old churches.
Massive oaken beams, embrowned by
smoke and centuries, cross the ceiling.
One compartment is further secluded by

JOHNSON'S SEAT, WITH PORTRAIT. "OLD CHESHIRE CHEESE."

By Seymour Lucas, R.A.

a dingy curtain, hung from a rod set a
foot or more above the top of the board
partition, and is known as "the cosey
corner."

Dr. Johnson's nook has wall-benches
on two sides ; a third side is made by the
projecting chimney, the table filling the
fourth that faces the room. Johnson's
portrait hangs above his bench. A brass
plate is let into the wall, testifying that
this was "the favourite seat of Dr. Samuel Johnson, *Born September 18, 1709.
Died December 13, 1784.*" Beneath a
pompous, eulogistic sentence we read one
more pithy and interesting :

"No, sir ! there is nothing which has
yet been contrived by man, by which so
much happiness has been produced, as by
a good tavern."—JOHNSON.

The round spots of darker brown upon
the wainscot were made, it is said, by
the loll of Johnson's greasy wig and the
restless rubbing of Goldsmith's head, as
they hobnobbed daily over roast, steak,
and home-brewed ale. The sawdust on
the floor is an indifferent substitute for

the sand that formerly coated and protected it.   Midway between door and
chimney is an iron umbrella-rack, the box-
bottom of which is filled with sawdust.
It has especial fascination for us, some-
how.   Johnson's umbrella, that must have
been big and baggy, and Goldsmith's,
that, most likely, had a broken rib and a
slit or two (if he owned one at all), leaned
against that frame times without number.
We easily conjure up the bear-like roll
and ponderous tread of the great lexi-
cographer up the aisle, until he flings
himself upon the creaking bench, poor
Oliver following with his dog-trot and his
bright, wistful eyes.   We hope and believe that, when he had not what "Young
America" calls "the price of a dinner"
in his pocket, he dined at Bruin's ex-
pense.

Charles II. consistently defied the pro-
prieties and amused his royal self by
bringing Nell Gwynne here to sup one
night after the play.   Discarding as apoc-
ryphal the tale that Shakespeare used to
take his chop and cup of sack at one of

these tables while his plays were " on " at
the Blackfriars Theatre, we yet remind
one another, whisperingly, that Robert
Herrick wrote to Ben Jonson of

> " these lyric feasts
> Made at The Sun,
> THE CHEESE, the Triple Tun " ;

that "the marvellous Boy," Chatterton,
loafed into the classic precincts to warm
his famishing body, and to bask his
hungrier soul and heart in the blaze of
the congregated wits. Alexander Pope,
Alfred Tennyson, David Garrick, John
Leech, Thomas Hood, Charles Dickens,
Edmund Burke, Thackeray, Voltaire,
Christopher North, Charles Matthews,
Douglas Jerrold, John Forster, Nathan-
iel Hawthorne, Sir Joshua Reynolds,—
what care we how we violate synchro-
nisms in our breathless enumeration of
a few of the shining host that have sat
upon these hard benches, eaten from
these clumsy tables, and made the smoke-
dyed rafters ring with debate and laugh-
ter? Epigrams were born in the old

eating-house as butterflies are evolved from cocoons by sunshine and summer airs. A catalogue of the noted *bons mots* here uttered for the first time would fill a fair-sized volume.

We have abundant leisure for memory and for thought, for, mistaking the hour at which THE PUDDING, the event of the day, would be served, we have forty-five minutes upon our hands. The waiter who spreads our white cloth and sets in array the willow-pattern plates, the caster, salt-cellars, cutlery, and pewter tankards, informs us in the husky sub-tone that befits hour and scene, that " IT will not be down until 'arf-parst one, to the minnit."

" The kitchen is upstairs, then ? "

" As it halways 'as been, sir. And IT 'as been done to a turn at 'arf-past one o'clock to the minnit for a 'undred years and more."

As the minutes pass, the room fills. No questions are asked ; no orders are given. For a while, the hum of voices from the bar trickles into the silence. This is hushed presently, and the five or

STAIRCASE IN "OLD CHESHIRE CHEESE."

From an Original Drawing by Herbert Railton.

six men who have loitered there enter
with the careful step of church-comers to
take the few remaining vacant seats.
Watches are furtively consulted when the
minutes have dwindled into seconds.   Still
there is no exhibition of restlessness. Ver-
ily, these English know how to wait for
what they are sure of getting.   In the hun-
dred-years-and-more they have learned that
IT is not to be hurried.

Four waiters appear, laden with immense piles of hot plates of generous
amplitude, and deposit them upon a table
near the door.   Two respectable and
ruddy Britons in the box adjoining ours
take off the hats they had not thought it
worth while to remove out of respect to
their fellow-guests.   Upon the heels of
the plate-bearers march two men with four
covered tureens of gravy.   These flank
the hot plates, leaving the upper end of
the board clear.   Then, a man walks in
quietly and takes his stand before the
vacant space.   From his dress-coat he
might be a Chief Butler.   From his handsome face, clean-shaven but for a mus-

tache, he might be an educated gentleman.   His deportment is that of a High
Priest, and the table is his altar.   An
attendant hands him a glittering knife and
a fork.

Our fingers and toes tingle; electric
shivers play up and down our spines in
the interval of perhaps thirty seconds that
elapses before there looms up in the doorway a big waiter, bearing aloft upon a
pair of muscular arms—

THE PUDDING.

He moves with judicious circumspec-
tion.   We recall, with a pang as swift
and keen as a jumping toothache, that
once—a generation or so ago—a hapless
predecessor of the Hercules tripped upon
the threshold in the supreme moment of
the Occasion, and let the Pudding fall.

It is safe to-day, albeit the table actually
groans as it is set down.   The gleaming
carver is raised—not with a flourish, as it
might be in the hands of a meaner artist
—and sinks into the full bosom, swelling
above the rim of the mammoth basin.   Slow

clouds of incense rise and soon pervade
the remotest corners.   The phlegmatic
Britons about us do not turn a hair.   Yet
their mouths must be watering behind
their clenched teeth.   Distribution, like
carving, is regulated by immutable rules.
Each expectant must take his turn.
Every plate is heaped, yet the only accompaniment of the Pudding is great
potatoes, smoking hot, that crumble into
meal at a touch.

If there can be two supreme moments
in the gastronomic Function at which we
are assisting, the second is that in which
we taste, for the first time, the Dish, the
fame of which has followed the British
drum-beat around the world.

It signifies next to nothing to say that
the crust, three inches thick, is as light as
a sponge and as tender as the heart of a
newly made widower; that beneath this
crust—embalmed in, and informed by, a
brown gravy of ineffable and indescribable
spiciness and savouriness, and as rich and
smooth as Alderney cream—are cubes of
juicy beefsteak and minute morsels of

marrow, larks, mushrooms, kidneys, and oysters, each, by some miracle of culinary genius, retaining its distinctive flavour, yet entering into and facilitating the accomplishment of a harmonious Whole.

Having satisfied ourselves as to these particulars by critical analysis, after the ecstasy of fruition is somewhat dulled by indulgence, we are as far as ever from grasping the mystery of proportion and concoction.

Custom, audited by common sense, ordains that THE PUDDING be washed down by "a pint of bitter." Which, being interpreted, is the mildest and mellowest of "brown October ale." It has consorted with the savoury Wonder for so long that divorce would be an outrage.

"Stewed Cheshire" is the one and only other course prescribed by tradition and appetite when the second—or, mayhap, the third—help of pudding has been declined—or, what is more likely, eaten. "Stewed Cheshire" is a kind of glorified Welsh rarebit, served in the square, shallow tins in which it is cooked, and gar-

"THE COZY CORNER" IN "OLD CHESHIRE CHEESE."

By Seymour Lucas, R.A.

nished with sippets of delicately coloured toast.

On the way out, we halt at the altar. The still steaming basin is three-quarters empty. In case some abnormally capacious customer should accept a fourth portion, the High Priest still holds the knife, but lightly, and resting, as it were, upon his arms. Rashly, being ignorant of his real rank, we accost him civilly, extol the Pudding, and inquire further into the antecedents thereof. He is courteous, and, for a High Priest, communicative.

The basin, or bowl, in which the pudding is cooked, stands eighteen inches high, and is twenty inches in diameter at the brim. It holds one hundred pounds of mixture, including the crust, and is boiled twenty hours. The recipe is a state secret, and the landlord keeps the formula in his safe when not using it. The Pudding is compounded in a locked room, then committed for boiling to a confidential cook.

"The Cheese," as the ancient hostelry is familiarly termed by affectionate *habit-*

ués, has been in the Moore family for several generations, descending, like a dukedom, from father to son. This we had heard prior to our visit. Not until we were quitting the storied spot did we discover that the suave High Functionary with whom we had been talking was Mr. Charles Moore, the present proprietor. He is a Churchwarden and a Common Councilman, with prospects of the Lord Mayoralty, should he care to have the office, a man of rare intelligence and culture.

The venerable eating-house has been a mine of wealth to his canny forbears and to himself. In nothing have they proved themselves more canny than in resisting what their revered Johnson anathematised as " the fury of innovation " that has transformed other chop-houses, The Mitre, The Dog, The Tun, and The Cock,—"most ancient of Taverns,"—into nineteenth-century restaurants, bereft of quaintness and tradition by new methods and new men, and has substituted cheap replicas for a Unique.

V

NO. 24 CHEYNE ROW

V

NO. 24 CHEYNE ROW

WE have asked to see the kitchen, first of all.

For the thought of Jane Welsh Carlyle, more than the fame of her husband, has brought us to No. 24—formerly No. 5—Cheyne Row (*Anglicé*, " Chain-ie ").

The kitchen is in what the English call " a sunken basement," with two half-windows opening across an area upon the street. A heavy deal table is in the middle of the floor. The dresser is the same in which Jane Welsh arranged her crockery with the help of Bessy Barnet, her one maid-servant, in the leafy month of June, 1834.

Bessy Barnet washed dishes in the ancient sink in the corner by the pump. Jane was sharp with a kitchen-maid, thirty years later, for letting the pump-well go "irrecoverably dry," though how the catastrophe could have been averted is an English enigma to us. The notable housekeeper must have had unrecorded battles with dough and circumstance over the ugly table and the sulky-looking sink in the days when she "got up at half-past seven to prepare the coffee and bacon-ham for breakfast," after which meal she swept the parlour and blackened the grate before making her own bed. The kitchen—she named it "an inferno"—could never have been cheerful, even on bright days. In foggy weather the inmates must have been obliged to work by lamplight.

The vision of the trig figure stepping briskly from table to range and dresser is suddenly struck from the imagination by something the custodian is saying:

" He used to smoke in the kitchen every night. His chair stood *here*,"—designating a spot at the right of the hearth. " Tennyson was often here and smoked with him. *He* sat at the opposite side of the fire. You may have heard of the time

when they smoked for two hours one night
and neither of them spoke a word.   When
Tennyson got up to go home, Carlyle said,
—'Coom again, soon, Alfred. We 've had
an awfully graund evening together.'"

"Would n't Mrs. Carlyle allow them to
smoke upstairs?"

"I don't know about that.   But Carlyle
liked to sit over the kitchen fire with his
pipe.   He said he felt more at home here
than anywhere else."

As was but natural in the son of a Scottish peasant.

The picture of the dainty mistress of
the home—a lady born and bred, who
married the eccentric plebeian against
the advice of her friends, and, believing
in him, "worked like a servant, bore
poverty and suffering and put up with
his humours, which were extremely trying"
—comes to the front again with this reply.
We have our doubts and our beliefs,
based upon what we know of her house-
wifery and her husband's habits.

"In about a week, it seems to me, all
was swept and garnished, fairly habitable,

and continued incessantly to get itself polished, civilised and beautiful to a degree that surprised me," wrote Carlyle of this epoch. He was effusively just to her—when she had passed beyond the reach of human praise or blame.

Doubt has hardened into belief by the time we mount the narrow kitchen stairs to what was, for twenty years, the Carlyles' "parlour." Here they sat and talked, and quarrelled, and made up, and lived what part of their lives was common to the two. Mrs. Carlyle called it, in rural phrase, her "best room." Folding-doors connect it with the smaller room in which they took their meals.

"The little oval clock" (now a fixture on the wall above the staircase leading to the upper floor) "is on his bracket in the back-room, with the dining-room oval table," Carlyle writes to his brother. "It is here we sit in dewy morning sunshine, and breakfast on hot coffee and the best of bread-and-butter."

Back of the dining-room is "a china-room, or pantry, or I know not what," says another letter—"all shelved and fit to hold crockery for the whole street."

Such passages as these had prepared us to look for something semi-palatial in the House the proud lessee spells, always, with a capital H. There is a touch of pathos in the raptures of the new tenants over their abode, since it is an unconscious revelation of the bare simplicity of their former home-living.

"The House is eminent, antique, wainscoted to the very ceiling; broadish stair with massive balustrade, corniced, and as thick as one's thigh," is one of the husband's florid periods. The more practical wife is almost as enthusiastic:

"The house is a massive concern, **an** excellent lodgement of most antique physiognomy, all wainscoted, carved and queer-looking, roomy, substantial, commodious, with closets to satisfy any Bluebeard."

To our eyes, the *ci-devant* "No. 5" is a very ordinary affair—a commonplace tenement in a middle-class Row; moderate in size and plain in finish, with nothing to commend it to our notice except the fact that for two-and-thirty years it housed a Genius, and was kept by his much-enduring wife.

By-and-by, as fame increased, and the family purse was heavier, important changes were made in the room above the humble "parlour." Up to now it had been Carlyle's study. *The French Revolution, Cromwell, Latter-Day Tracts*, and many of his lectures were written here. In 1852 was begun the work of "an enlargement of it into a kind of Drawing-room according to modern ideas," as Carlyle put it. Jane meant it for a library, where he could continue to write, yet where visitors might be received in a style somewhat suitable to their rising fortunes.

But the nest was stirred. The "excellent, large, wholesome apartment, in size 19 by 18 feet," in which, Carlyle tells his brother, he is trying to work, was soon condemned as untenantable. Much humouring of his moods and tenses had made him more "notional" than ever.

CARLYLE'S ATTIC STUDY.

"For three days his satisfaction over the rehabilitated house lasted; on the fourth the young lady next door took a fit of practising upon her accursèd pianoforte, and he started up, disenchanted, in his new library and informed heaven and earth in a peremptory manner that there he could neither think nor live, that the carpenter must be brought back, and steps taken to make him a quiet place anywhere—perhaps, best of all, on the roof of the house."

The volcanic upheaval gave Jane the long-sighed-for drawing-room. There were portraits upon the walls, presented by noble friends, Albert Dürer engravings, and rare prints; two pier-glasses were between the windows, and a square mirror was over the mantel. Sofas and chairs were grouped with tables and piano; a Bramah grate was set in blue tiles; burners superseded lamps, and gold-plated candlesticks, silver and green lacquered bronze statuettes, made a show that excited the envy of plainer neighbours. Mrs. Carlyle was "justly proud of the room,"

says a chronicler.   She had not a tithe of
the genuine comfort in it she had known
in the old-fashioned "parlour" on the
ground-floor.

A picture painted by Robert Tait for
Lord Ashburton shows the Carlyles at
home in this, the "best room" of their
earlier days.   Carlyle, in his plaided dress-
ing-gown, pipe in hand, one of his great
feet crossed at the ankle over the other,
leans against the corner of the mantel.
Jane sits in an arm-chair on the other end
of the rug, serene and matronly, her chin
supported by her hand.   The round table
is strewed with books and papers; through
the wide folding-doors we see the dining-
room, the floor of which, like that of the
"parlour," is covered with the carpet from
the Craigenputtock drawing-room, "sup-
plemented by a border."   The cage of
"Chico," the wonderful canary, is on a
stand near the open door of the china-
room.   Nero, Mrs. Carlyle's pet dog, the
"infatuated little beast" who took kindly
to Carlyle, lies, fat and fluffy, upon a sofa.

All for comfort, and nothing too fine

for daily use—is the story told by the apartment where the piquante, shrewd, busy, and usually sunny-faced, wee hostess received her husband's friends as her own. Leigh Hunt, who lived just around the corner, dropped in every evening, "always rather scrupulously, though most simply and modestly dressed." A "Kind of Talking Nightingale," Mrs. Carlyle called him. She played Scotch tunes on the piano for him, and they read Burns together; then she listened to his singing and playing until the supper of oatmeal-porridge was served. He always took a tiny bowl of it, and, after sugaring it, sipped it from a tea-spoon delicately, in bird-like fashion. His wife borrowed daily and hourly from Mrs. Carlyle's kitchen,—tumblers, tea-cups, a spoonful of tea, a cupful of meal,—"not having a copper in her purse."

Thither came John Stuart Mill, and Mazzini, with Count Pepoli and other refugees, and John and Anthony Sterling, and Froude and Forster, and dozens of other *notabilia*, to admire Carlyle and to

fall in love, straightway, with his wife, as
she sat a queen among "her dainty bits
of arrangement, ornamentations, all so
frugal, simple, full of grace, propriety and
ingenuity, as they ever were." Between
this and the dining-room stood the four-
leaved screen, five feet high, that kept her
busy for many weeks, "pasting it all over
with prints."

"It will be a charming work of art when
finished," she says, merrily.

Carlyle's *post-mortem* foot-note is,—
"Stands here to this day, the beautifullest
and cleverest screen I have ever seen.
How strange, how mournfully affecting to
me, now!"

Especially how "strange"! The
chances are that he never gave it a glance
while she lived.

Edward Irving—her early lover and,
according to some, her love, as well—saw
her in this room, one month before his
death, and a smile lit up his wan eyes as
he said,—"You are an Eve, making a little Paradise wherever you are."

Ah me! the might-have-beens that stare

and gape upon us in this crooked, every-
day world of ours!

We like best—and most nearly love—
Jane Welsh Carlyle here, and find it in
our housewifely hearts to forgive her for
letting her lumbering Craigenputtock boor
smoke his black pipe and incubate his
sublime and sullen fancies, for two immortal hours, before the kitchen fire.

In all those early years she was a brave
little hypocrite, deluding herself with
others, jotting down pleasant and pious fic-
tions for her old mother-in-law, of her con-
tentment with her matrimonial "bargain."

"I could wish him a little less yellow,
and a little more peaceable—but that is
all," she affirms within a year after their
removal to the Cheyne Row Paradise.
She usually meant what she said at the
time, and meant some things too strenu-
ously for her own happiness and her husband's comfort.

It is idle to attempt disguise of the truth
that she changed her mind and her feelings materially with the passage of years,
and the widening of her world.

" The most intimate friend she had in
the world " makes no pretences of this
sort in commenting upon what was out-
wardly the most prosperous period of the
badly joined lives :

" She was miserable at this time ; more
abidingly and intensely miserable than
words can utter. . . . Mr. Carlyle once said
to me that she ' had the deepest and tenderest feelings, but narrow.'   Any other
wife would have laughed at his bewitch-
ment with Lady Ashburton, but to her
there was a complicated aggravation that
made it hard to endure.   She was making daily, hourly endeavours that his life
should be as free from hindrances as possible.   He put her aside for his work, but
lingered in the ' Primrose path of dalli-
ance ' for the sake of a great lady who
liked to have a philosopher in chains.   Bear
in mind that her life was solitary—no tenderness, no caresses, no loving words ;
nothing out of which one's heart can make
the wine of life.   A glacier on a mountain
would have been as human a companionship."

" My Man-of-Genius-Husband," Jeannie
calls the glacier, sportively, with a dash of
bitterness in sparkle and foam.   At this
time she began the journal the Man-of-
Genius's worshippers blame Mr. Froude
for publishing.   What would you have ?
Misery cannot be forever silent, and paper
was a safer confidante than even the " most
intimate friend I have in the world."

" That eternal Bath House !" is an entry under date of October 21, 1855.   " I
wonder how many thousand miles Mr. Carlyle has walked between here and there,
putting it all together ; setting up one mile-
stone and another betwixt himself and
me ! "

A more characteristic note is jotted
down on November 5th.

" Alone this evening.   Lady A. in town
again, and Mr. C. of course at Bath House.

> " When I think of what I is
> And what I used to was,
> I 'gin to think I 've sold myself
> For very little cas."

Plucky and wretched wee wifie !   She

gives a comical turn to her very misery,
as one grimaces under torture to keep
from screaming.

We are wofully out of sympathy with
hero-worship while we glance at the mod-
ernised drawing-room, pause reverently in
Mrs. Carlyle's bedchamber behind it, and
then visit the sound-proof folly that takes
in the whole attic-story. With all its ridiculous contrivances it cost the never rich
couple one thousand dollars, "turning out
to be," as Jane bemoans herself to a cor-
respondent, "the noisiest apartment in the
house."

We laugh in looking about us at the
ventilators that collect and echo sound
and reject fresh air; the front and back
windows filled with ground glass to exclude sights from without; the skylight
that must act like a burning-glass in hot
weather. It is an ungainly and comfortless den,—literally a waste and howling
wilderness. Carlyle set his Scotch jaw
grimly and finished *Frederick the Great*
here, nevertheless, then transferred writ-
ing-desk and books to the dining-room on

the ground-floor, where he worked until his death.

The garden at the back of the house is thickset with associations of our heroine. The "two vines which produced two bunches of grapes in the season" still cling to the wall. The stump alone remains of the walnut-tree from which she gathered "almost sixpence worth of walnuts." In the extreme left-hand angle of the wall is the pear-tree to which, while the house was in repairing, she lashed "a gypsy's tent, constructed out of clothes-ropes and posts and the crumb-cloth of the library," and sat under it with her work, meanwhile superintending carpenters and painters.

Her widower did some hard thinking in the garden over his "final pipe" and under the stars, when his "heroic, lovely, pathetic, noble and beautiful darling" had "left him, as it were, in her car of heaven's fire."

"HER little Gooseberry-bush, her Hawthorn, Ash-tree, &c., are in vigorous bud again, almost in leaf in this Patch of

Garden," he sentimentalises in his journal, two years after her death, heedful of his capitals in the midst of his grief. "Nor are these sad remembrances without some use to me ; solemn, high and beautiful, like the Gates of Eternity, with a light as of stars."

We exchange uncharitable views as to the depth of the remorse expressed in syllabical sobs between, and as foot-notes of, letters that for spicy humour, crispness, play of fancy, and depth of feeling have not their equals in the range of English literature. In her garden, our hearts burn within us with a passion of pity.

The custodian pauses on her way back to the house, and looks over her shoulder :

"You will please observe that there is no side or back entrance to the kitchen. All household supplies, even coals, were brought in at the front door, carried along the hall, and so down to the basement. *That* must have been a trial to a 'particular' housekeeper like Mrs. Carlyle. As to her other troubles "—forsaking the per-

CARLYLE'S HOUSE AND GARDEN.

" The garden is thickset with associations.'

functory tone for one that strikes us as suspiciously earnest—"there are many, many wives who have just as bad—and worse—and the world is none the wiser. The difference is that she made such an outcry over her tribulations that, after all, were n't so peculiar and exceptional as she imagined.   I 'm not denying that he was a hard man to live with, but if she had held her tongue, it would have been better for his reputation—and maybe for her own.   If there was mustard in his temper, there was cayenne, and plenty of it, in hers."

6

VI

DANTE'S EVERY-DAY WIFE

VI

DANTE'S EVERY-DAY WIFE

HER name was, of course, not Beatrice. Neither did Petrarch marry Laura, nor Werther his bread-and-butter Charlotte. Mrs. Unwin never became Mrs. William Cowper, Michael Angelo worshipped, without espousing, Vittoria Colonna, and Pocahontas wedded the prosy widower, John Rolfe, instead of giving her delicate, tawny hand to the other John whose life she had the habit of saving.

For half an hour we have been roaming in and out of the loops and angles of alleys that did active duty as streets in the Florence of 1265, and which, unto this day, have resisted the broadening and straightening propensities of modern engineers. Proconsolo, Pandolfini, degli Albizzi, S. Martino, and half-a-score of other " Vias,"

intersect and zigzag as the Makers of Florence willed, and remain a joy forever to
the dreamer and historian.

The reputed birthplace of Dante in the
obscure Via S. Martino cowers in the shadow of an ambitious tower built for the
tenancy of the foreign governors of the
city.   It passed into the possession of a
private family before the great poet was
born. *La Casa di Dante* may, or may
not, be the same as that occupied by his
parents and himself.   The site and the environs suffice to feed our fancies.   About
a stone's cast away from the home of the
Alighieri, and what would be just " around
the corner," if the Via obeyed just and
rectilinear rules, lived Folco Portinari,
father of the Beatrice whose name jingles
as accordantly with Dante's as Adam's
with Eve's.   This house has also been
pulled *at*, if not down, and reconstructed
into a palace.   The court was unaltered
in the renovations, and to the right, as
one enters from the street, is " Dante's
Niche " (*Nicchia di Dante*) where the love-
lorn boy of Portinari's neighbour made a

fixture of himself by the hour upon the
chance of seeing his divinity flit by him,
on her way in, or out, of her home.   While
lingering and watching here, he composed
the *Vita Nuova*—" a fantastic, delicious
record, as pure and sweet as it is vision-
ary," as one appreciative critic has said.
In the innocent frolic indulged in by the
boys and girls of the neighbourhood after
a *festa* given by Folco Portinari, the nine-
year-old Dante met, perhaps joined hands
in the games with, Beatrice, a pretty girl
of eight.   It is hardly possible that he saw
her then for the first time, but his eyes were
suddenly unsealed by some subtle chrism,
to behold in her his fate for time and
eternity.

"Her dress was of a most noble colour,"
—he writes with naïveté that makes us
smile—"a subdued and becoming crimson, and she wore a cincture and ornaments befitting her childish years."

A *catalogue raisonné* of ribbons, sash,
and jewels would be an interesting item
in the history of thirteenth-century mil-
linery.

"From that time forth Love held sovereign empire over my soul," he adds in
earnest good faith, Love and Beatrice
becoming henceforward interchangeable
terms.   He forthwith built a bower in
his soul, and invited her in thought, never
by word or glance, to dwell therein with
him.   He seems, moreover, to have been
measurably satisfied with such sublimated
companionship for another nine years.
Then, as one awakening from a vague,
sweet dream, the watcher in the niche had
a second apparition of "the wonderful
creature."

"She appeared to me in white robes,
between two ladies who were older than
she ; and, passing by the street, she turned
her eyes toward that place where I stood
very timidly, and in her ineffable courtesy
saluted me so graciously that I seemed
then to see the heights of all blessedness."

For all the dual chaperonage that
guarded the eighteen-year-old beauty, she
thus contrived to convey to her adorer
her consciousness of that which must have
flattered her, if it kindled no warmer

emotion.   Boccaccio gives us more than
one intimation that Dante's timid worship
would have been graciously approved had
it been many degrees less "timid."   At
their former meeting, "the child turned
her gaze from time to time upon Dante
with so much tenderness as filled the boy
brimful with delight."

By and by, she ceased to notice him in
passing, by so much as a glance—"having heard, as was supposed, evil tales of
him."   A gratuitous supposition, to our
way of looking at the matter.   Nine years
was a long time, even in that patient age,
for a pretty girl to wait for a "declara-
tion."   His soul exhaled in poetical sighs,
but he continued to stand by "very
timidly," and asked no questions.

At twenty, Beatrice Portinari married
Simone di Bardi, a husband designated
by her parents, an incident that in no wise
altered her mystic relations with the dumb
lover.   As philosophically as tunefully he
says that "the Lord Love has placed all
my happiness in that which cannot be
taken from me."   To the public and to

her legal spouse, she seemed to dwell in Simone di Bardi's house. To the clarified senses of her spirit-lover, she was ever his "own most gentle lady," and filled the bower he had built with the radiance of her presence.

For four years after her marriage, "the wonderful creature, crowned and clothed in humility," trod these strait streets, seeming not to hear the murmurs that followed her passing: "This is not a woman, but one of the most beautiful angels of heaven." Then she died, and Dante Alighieri joined hands with her in perpetual companionship, and walked with her in Paradise.

The story is immortal, a miracle of passion that was all flame, yet all purity, of constancy to an ideal on which Disillusion never laid a profaning finger.

Yet our hearts are soft, as after a fall of spring rain, with thoughts of another woman, concerning whom the poet has not left a line so much as to tell us that she ever lived and was seen by him, and to whom his biographers have not cared to award the honour denied her by the husband.

In 1293—three years after the death of Simone di Bardi's wife—Dante married, in the dingy little church of S. Martino, hard by the *Casa di Dante*, Gemma, a daughter of Manetti Donati, a wealthy and powerful Florentine. Her family was superior to that of the Alighieri in social and political standing, but they were neighbours and friends, and young Dante had known Gemma from her childhood. It is quite within the probabilities that she may have borne her part in the games through which Beatrice glided in the noble-coloured gown set off by becoming sash and trinkets. The marriage was evidently agreeable to both sides of the house. Dante complimented one of his brothers-in-law by allotting to him a respectable position in Paradise, and is, himself, saluted there by the shade as "sweet brother." In short, the connection was eminently suitable in the eyes of relations, friends, and gossips in general, and, so far as we can judge, a willing bridegroom led a willing bride to the altar of the shabby little church we now enter.   A dark, stifling nook we find it, pervaded by an odour that may be the fumes of incense a hundred years old, and much the worse for keeping.   If it was no larger then than at present, the kins-people of Alighieri and Donati must have overflowed it and the street, on the wed-ding-day, six hundred years ago.

Was Gemma among the gentlewomen (*gentili donne*)—" some of whom had been present at my misfortunes "—who pitied and sought to console him at Beatrice's marriage, and again at her death?   One of these fair and sympathetic acquaint-ances ran to her lattice to look down upon the youth of the clear-cut profile and fathomless eyes, who wrote love-verses and had won his spurs upon the bloody field of Campaldino, and who, al-though but twenty-five, was already spoken of by one faction as a turbulent citizen who might prove dangerous some day, and by the other as a rising man.   This was six months before Dante's marriage.

CHURCH OF SAN MARTINO, IN WHICH DANTE WAS MARRIED.

He caught sight of the pitying face bent
upon him, and her glance was a drop of
balm upon his still sore heart.   If he (or
she) followed up the advantage afforded
by the accident, he was too much engrossed by the *Vita Nuova* and Florentine politics to write down the fact.

We know absolutely nothing of Madonna Gemma's personal appearance, temper, taste, or habits.   If she wore a
flame-coloured gown when Dante asked
her hand in marriage, or white when they
stood side by side in the wee church
where their fathers worshipped—nobody
took the pains to mention these insignifi-
cant details.   She looked after her house
— probably her father's wedding-present—
and her husband's diet and clothes, and,
at the end of seven otherwise unrecorded
years, had added seven children to the
furniture of their home, and named, or let
the father name, one of their daughters
" Beatrice."

We are disposed to lay more stress upon
this circumstance than the christening of
one child in so large a family would seem

to demand.   The mother was not jealous of her beautiful early playfellow, and was cognisant of her lord's Platonic espousals to the companion of his soul-wanderings in other worlds than ours. Perhaps— poor, simple soul!—she juggled, and, as she thought, artfully, to win a morsel of the sweet loaf of affectionate commendation for the pretty tribute to his spirit-bride. He had vowed, when Beatrice died, "to say that of her which was never yet said of any woman," and he fulfilled the vow, dreaming and writing of her, and weeping over what he had written, while Gemma bore and managed their children, and made purchases in the *Mercato Vecchio*, and went to church on Sundays and holy-days to pray that his ambition and stiff principles might not get him into trouble with the State.

So Poe kept tryst with "Lost Lenore," while Virginia Clemm, his every-day wife, was dying of slow starvation in the next room of the fireless Fordham cottage.

In 1301, Dante left Florence on an embassy to Rome, lingering there, at the

request of the Pope, until a Florentine
revolution made it impossible for him to
return to his city and home.   Corso Donati, Gemma's brother, was her husband's
political enemy, but he extended a grudg-
ing protection to his sister and her seven
babies after Dante was banished and pro-
scribed.   Her house, close to the church
of S. Martino, was no longer a safe place
in which to keep valuables that might
tempt the cupidity of roving bands of
depredators, eager for news of anything
belonging to a confiscated estate.   Gemma
had been sole guardian of household goods
and of children during her husband's year
of absence, and was too familiar with
émeutes to be taken by surprise by the
latest overthrow.   Family friends offered
to keep her portable treasures until such
time as it would be safe for her to reclaim
them.   She gathered up and packed in
stout coffers whatever she considered most
precious, and consigned them to acquaint-
ances less liable to suspicion than herself.

We see coffers every day in "antiquity"
lumber-rooms in dark, out-of-the-rush quar-

ters of the town, roomy, and banded with iron or steel, any one, or six, of which may have served our thrifty house-mother at that troublous epoch.

Six years afterward, when a calmer period intervened, before the outburst of another revolution, Madonna Gemma deputed her husband's favourite nephew to overhaul one of the strong boxes. It was filled with papers of all sorts, collected in her husband's study. The young fellow, burrowing in the confused mass in idle, affectionate curiosity, happened presently upon manuscripts in his uncle's well known handwriting, poems and *canzoni*, "and among the rest which pleased him most was a *quadernetto*, in which were written, in Dante's own hand, the first seven cantos of what appeared to him a very beautiful thing."

Dante's biographers assume that his wife guessed nothing of the value of papers, that, when restored to the exiled poet, grew under his hand into the *Inferno*. If they are right, the more credit belongs to her for the love that prompted

the preservation of every scrap of parch-
ment his pen had touched.   They were
hoarded—because they were his, and not
for their intrinsic worth—along with her
silver, jewels, and title-deeds.   A selfish
woman would have left them where they
lay, upon shelves and tables the master
had not seen in twelve months. A woman
without sentiment would have burned
them as waste-paper.

" Since it has pleased God that it should
not be lost, but sent back to me, I will do
my best to follow up the work according
to my first intention," was the pious acknowledgment of the author to the Provi-
dence that had restored his manuscript to
him.

He was ready to ascribe praise to the
Great Giver of the unexpected good.
There was no word then, or ever, for
God's humble instrument in the work of
preservation.   The world that cherishes
his noblest poem as a perpetual heritage
does not look back to the means by which
it was transmitted to us.

Before the discovery of the priceless

rough draught of the seven cantos, Gemma
had sent her eldest born, Pietro, a lad of
thirteen, to cheer his father's loneliness in
Bologna, and—we cannot but surmise—
with some faint hope that her husband's
heart would turn longingly to home and
her for that in the boy's face and voice
that recalled her younger and blither self.
Pietro studied with his father during
Dante's two years' sojourn in the university town, and accompanied him in wanderings that ended in Ravenna, "the
melancholy old city, old even in Dante's
day." A second son, Jacopo, was consigned by his mother to the expatriated
father, a few years after his brother left
Florence. Whatever were the mitiga-
tions of his banishment which the two
brought, Dante's heart yearned and sick-
ened unto deathly faintness for "the most
beautiful and most famous daughter of
Rome, Firenza." "A bark without sail
and without helm," his passionate love
for the peerless Tuscan city was a magnet
that continually drew his thoughts toward
her. Even after he found a pleasant asy-

DANTE ALIGHIERI, FROM THE FRESCO BY GIOTTO, FLORENCE.

" The youth with the clear-cut profile and fathomless eyes."

lum and kind friends in Ravenna, he
passed whole days in the balsamic boski-
ness of her pine groves, "thinking of
Florence and civil wars, and meditating
cantos of his poem."

Be assured that if the name of Gemma,
or of the young daughters, fast growing
to womanhood, ever passed his lips or
escaped from his pen, we should have
heard of it.   If he pined for home it was
because that home was in Firenza, not
because Firenza was home.

Madonna Gemma Alighieri never looked
again into the deep eyes and upon the classic face whose beauty had captivated and
held her heart.   The exile drew his last
sigh in Ravenna in 1321, a homesick pilgrim to the close of his fifty-six years,
dreaming hopelessly, almost in the death-
hour, of return to his native country, and
of "hiding his white hairs beneath the
leaves" of the laureate's crown bestowed
by repentant compatriots.

"And there can be no doubt," we state
upon the authority of Boccaccio, "that he
was received into the arms of his most no-

ble Beatrice, with whom, in the presence of Him Who is the Chief Good, leaving all miseries of the present life, they now most lightsomely live in that happiness to which there comes no end."

Dante had foreseen, in beatific vision, this apotheosis a quarter-century before.

" May it please Him, Who is the Lord of courtesy, that my soul may see the glory of my lady, that blessèd Beatrice, who gloriously beholds His face."

We find no entry anywhere of Gemma's death, or if she were wife or widow when she and the working-day world parted company. Pietro and Jacopo left Ravenna after their father's death, and became two gentlemen of Verona under the patronage of a noble friend of Dante. Alive or dead, their mother had no hold upon their allegiance. They were weaned from her and from Florence.

We never pass the Piazza Santa Croce without pausing to look at the statue of Dante in the centre of the square. It was set here when he had been dead five hundred and forty-four years.

" Florence now to love him is content,"
is the tardy congratulation of an Anglo-
Italian poet.   There is a suggestion, in
the statue, of the haughty disdain we can
imagine the hunted exile might have felt
had he been foretold, in dying, of the posthumous tribute.   One nervous hand has
gathered up his robe, as from contact with
the dust of the city that barred her gates
and her heart against him, and now ranks
him among her gods.   About the pedestal
the Florentine lions hold up to the specta-
tor shields lettered with the titles of his
famous works.   Conspicuous among them
is that of the *Vita Nuova*, wherein he re-
deemed his pledge to the shade of the
" blessèd Beatrice," and the far nobler *Inferno*, saved to him and to posterity by
the housewifely thrift and single-hearted
devotion of his Every-Day Wife.

VII

THE PROPHET OF SAN MARCO

VII

THE PROPHET OF SAN MARCO

IT is a solemn shade that has walked with us all through the forenoon of this April day. A shade with a visage as sad as was his life, as stern as his death, has moved at our side. From the Duomo, which was thronged for six years with Florentines of every grade of society and order of intellect, to listen to the Preacher-monk of San Marco,—along streets twisting between cliff-like walls which echoed to his footsteps, four hundred years agone, —to the now commonplace Piazza San Marco.

The plain façade of the Church and the low wings of the cloisters bound one side; more modern buildings, *pensiones* and shops, the other three. A hideous tramway enters the square at the side of the cloisters, and runs the entire length to the egress at the bottom of the open space. The centre of the quadrangle is planted with bushy palms and stubbly palmettoes, and out of the stiff and sombre greenery rises a semi-colossal statue of a modern Italian patriot, facing the street that bears the name of another hero of Young Italy.

On a day as balmy as this, about the beginning of Lent in 1498, the Piazza was packed to suffocation by a concourse of men and women, many kneeling, some standing, all with eyes fixed upon a solitary black-robed figure lifted far above their heads by a scaffold erected against the front wall of the Church.

The monk's cowl had fallen back from the upraised face; the noble head and draped figure stood out in bold relief against the pale blank behind him. At the full length of his right arm he held the Pyx above his head. In rising from his knees after a moment of silent prayer, he had spoken one sentence. The wonderful voice that had so often swayed the mixed multitude in the Duomo, pealed to the re-

motest outskirts of the square, a volume
of sound that might have fallen from the
vast hollow of the heavens above the
startled host. The excommunicated man
had already and publicly defied the thun-
ders of the Pontifical throne :

" He who has gained the Pontifical chair
by bribery is not Christ's Vicar. . . .
His commands are contrary to the Christian life. It is lawful to disobey them,"
were words that had shaken all Florence
and all Italy to superstitious trembling.
His challenge now was to High Heaven :

" If I have said anything to you, citizens
of Florence, in the name of God which
was not true ; if the Apostolical censure
pronounced against me is valid ;—*if I
have deceived anyone*—pray to God that
He will send fire from Heaven upon me
and consume me in presence of the people,—and I pray our Lord God, Three in
One, whose body I hold in this Blessed
Sacrament, to send death to me in this
place if I have not preached the truth."

Then, in the upper air where he stood,
and over the praying masses below, there

was silence about the space of half-an-hour
before Girolamo Savonarola descended
the pulpit steps and, attended by a procession of friars and acolytes, chanting a *Te
Deum*, returned to the Convent.

Still following the solemn shade, we
walk, seldom uttering a word, past what
was once the peaceful Convent garden,
where, in his earlier and happier days,
Savonarola gathered the novices, whom he
fondly called " our angels " (*i nostri angi-
oli*), in an arbour covered by damask roses,
—and so on, along corridors, and by cells
painted with "incomparable sweet angels,"
and other sacred subjects, by Fra Angel-
ico, upon his knees,—until we reach the
Prior's Cell. A portrait of Savonarola
from the brush of his trusty and well-
beloved Fra Bartolommeo, hangs against
the wall. It is hardly more distinct to our
bodily eyes than the shadowy visage we
have had with us all the morning. Rugged, uncomely, the heavily moulded features belying the tradition of his gentle
blood, and telling, more forcibly than his
pen has done, what battles the spirit

CELL OF SAVONAROLA IN CONVENT OF SAN MARCO.

waged with flesh and passion—it is yet
the face of a master among men, and a
conqueror to the end, even when that end
was a shameful death.

The resemblance to George Eliot, often
commented upon by those who have compared the two portraits, is the more striking to us now, for the circumstance that a
volume of *Romola* is our companion in this
day's round, and we have read the eloquent description of the friar's appeal to
Heaven, standing just where the shadow
of the pulpit and the gowned figure must
have fallen on that memorable morning.
His crucifix is here, his rosary, the hard
chair in which he sat at his desk, some
MSS.,—among them his sober and sensi-
ble argument against " The Trial by Fire,"
proposed, and afterward insisted upon, by
his Franciscan enemies,—his hair-cloth
shirt, and a bit of browned wood from
which we withdraw our eyes quickly.   It
was taken from the pile on which he was
burned to ashes in the Piazza della Signoria, at the will of the Florence he had
saved, over and again, from the power of

her enemies ; the fair Florence he sought, with his latest breath, to save from the worst of her foes, even her violent, dissolute, rapacious, and most ungrateful self.

There is one window in the Prior's Cell, and it differed in nothing from the comfortless niches occupied by his subordinates, except in the simple grandeur of him who tenanted it. In memory of what made that difference, we bend our heads in reverence, and our hearts swell to aching.

His farewell to Convent and Brotherhood, and to his " angels," was said in the vaulted library near the close of that very Lent ushered in by the scene in the Piazza which we have described. A mob, led by the vilest fellows of the parties opposed to Savonarola's endeavours to reform a corrupt Church and regulate a lawless State, attacked the Church of San Marco during the Vesper Service of Palm Sunday. The small congregation dispersed in terror, leaving the inmates of the Convent to support the fury of the assault. The monks attempted a brave, but vain, defence of their altar and their lives. Savonarola,

crucifix in hand, cast himself between the
rioters and his friends, and led the devoted little band out of the burning church
into the great library.   As calmly as if
they had been kneeling as usual for evening prayer and to receive his benediction,
he told them that the end of the long
struggle had come.

"I little thought that the whole city
would so soon have turned against me ;
but God's will be done !   My last admon-
ition to you is this—Let your arms be
Faith, Patience, and Prayer.   I leave you
with anguish and pain, to pass into the
hands of my enemies.   I know not whether
they will take my life.   But of this I am
certain,—that dead, I shall be able to do
far more for you in Heaven than living I
have ever had power to do for you on earth.
Be comforted, embrace the Cross, and by
that you will find the haven of salvation."

He threaded, for the last time, the familiar streets by the route we now take to
the Piazza della Signoria.   His hands
were bound tightly behind him ; the hoot-
ing, hustling populace followed so hard

after him that the pent-house made over
his head by the crossed pikes and swords
of the soldiery, whose orders were to bring
him to their masters alive, did not suffice
to ward off all blows and missiles. He was
dragged thus, battered and bleeding, and
more dead than alive, past the Duomo,
where, less than two years before, he had
preached to " more people than could get
into the Cathedral."

" They got up in the middle of the night,
and came to the door of the Cathedral,
waiting outside 'till it should be opened.
.   .   .   Then the silence was great in the
church, each one going to his place; and
he who could read, with a taper in his
hand, read the service and other prayers.
.   .   .   Thus they waited three or four
hours 'till the Padre (Savonarola) entered
the pulpit.   And the attention of so great
a mass of people, all with eyes and ears
attent upon the preacher, was wonderful.
They listened so, that when the sermon
reached its end, it seemed to them that
it had scarcely begun."

This had gone on for the eight years he

had foretold as the duration of his mighty work in that place.

Bruised, and we hope in mercy, stunned, the fallen Father (!) was carried across the great Piazza della Signoria, over the very spot covered in the Carnival of 1496 with the pyramidal bonfire of vanities collected by his regiment of converted *gamins*.

The reformer was then upon the top wave of popular favour. The effort " to get up the dear old masques and practical jokes, well spiced with indecency," was futile at that memorable *festa*.

" Such things were not to be tolerated in a city where Christ was declared King." The Florentine street-boys, the agents in the collection of dice, playing-cards, "masks and masquerading dresses; handsome copies of Ovid, Boccaccio, Petrarca, Pulci, and other books of a vain or impure sort; rouge-pots, false hair, mirrors, perfumes, powders, and transparent veils . . . and on the top of all, the symbolic figure of the old debauched Carnival,"—paraded the streets, "singing divine praises, and walking in white robes."

Their leader was watchful of them throughout.

"The Florentine youth had very evil habits and foul tongues. It seemed, at first, an unmixed blessing when they were got to shout, '*Viva Gesù!*' But Savonarola was forced to say, at last, from the pulpit: 'There is a little too much shouting of "*Viva Gesù!*" This constant utterance of sacred words brings them into contempt.'"

The coat-of-arms of the so-called "regenerate city" is carved upon the front of the Palazzo Vecchio—the letters "I. H. S." encircled by rays. It was not there when he who had, nevertheless, proclaimed his Lord and Master King of Florence, and of the Universe, was haled into the gates to prison and to torture.

We mount the hundreds of stone steps he was forced to climb while he could walk, up which he was borne by cursing jailors after each repetition of the tortures applied without pity and without stint.

"We have had to deal with a man of the most extraordinary patience of body and wisdom of soul, who hardened himself against all kinds of torture," wrote his judicial murderers to their Commander, the Pope of Rome, whom the "man" had defied. "Notwithstanding a long and most careful interrogatory, and with *all the help of torture*, we could scarcely extract anything out of him which he wished to conceal from us, although we laid open the inmost recesses of his mind."

In the intervals separating these various processes of laying open his mind, he was confined in the eyrie to which we have laboriously ascended,—the *Alberghettino*, a cell so strait that a tall man could hardly stretch himself in it. A mere slit of a window showed him a section of blue sky by day, a star or two by night. When they brought him in, fainting from the rack, they flung him upon the stone ledge that served him for a bed by night, a seat by day. The street sounds of the false city that had spewed him out of her mouth, came up to him like sighing breakers upon a distant shore. Here and thus he spent the Easter of 1498.

Pen and ink were always within his reach—left there with a purpose—and with devilish craft. With them he wrote "Meditations" upon such passages as "*Have mercy upon me, O God, according to Thy loving-kindness*," and "*Pull me out of the net that they have laid privily for me, for Thou art my strength.*" The rack had dislocated his left arm and wrist; the right hand was spared that he might affix a legible signature to his recantation.

Failing to extort this, they condemned him to die in the bonfire *(bel fuoco)* which his enemies had promised themselves and their associate demons should ere long light up the grey brows of the Palazzo Vecchio.

He passed his last night of pain, by gracious and special permission of the Signoria, in the hall on a lower floor (*the Sala dei Cinquecento*). It had been enlarged under Savonarola's own superintendence to accommodate two thousand citizens, should they wish to converse upon affairs of State. He had preached here several times, in the days when his

word was law as well as gospel, to his
fickle hearers, and upon the wall were
lettered words dictated by himself—of
which this is a poor translation :

> " If this great council and sure government,
>   O people ! of thy city, never cease
>   To be by these preserved, as by God sent,
>   In freedom shalt thou ever stand, and peace."

The two friars who were also to die on
the morrow were with him, and they
talked together until his strength gave
out, of what they were to endure, and what
lay beyond. As their Master had not
protested His innocence upon the Cross,
he said to them, neither should they speak
to the people to-morrow. It would soon
be over now, and so he bade " God bless
them," and " Good-night," before falling
asleep with his head in the lap of the
younger of the two.

At sunrise, they partook of their last
Sacrament, and repeated together their
last Confession of Faith. On their way
along the platform stretched from the
Palazzo to the gallows and funeral pyre

erected over there in the square, Savonarola was overheard by his executioners
repeating to himself: "*I believe in God,
the Father Almighty, Maker of Heaven
and earth, and in Jesus Christ, His Only
Son, our Lord*," and so on to the close of
the Creed.

For three-hundred-and-odd years the
women of Florence used to resort to the
Piazza della Signoria to lay flowers upon
the spot where rested the gallows' foot on
the 23d of May, 1498, in grateful memory
of the prophet whom their fathers had
killed.

"In Heaven," said a successor of the
Pope who ordered the deed, "I shall
know the explanation of three great mys-
teries—the Immaculate Conception, the
suppression of the Society of Jesus, the
death of Savonarola. . . . Saint, schis-
matic, or heretic, ignorant vandal or Christian artist, prophet, or charlatan, champion
of the Roman Church, or apostle of eman-
cipated Italy—which was Savonarola?"

The Church by whose Infallible Head
he was brought to the torture-chamber and

PALAZZO VECCHIO, FLORENCE.

Where Savonarola was imprisoned, and in front of which he was burned.

the scaffold, and the world that was not worthy of him, give a tardy answer.

A certain Monseigneur, a Lord Cardinal, interested himself actively in a celebration of the four hundredth anniversary of Savonarola's " martyrdom." There were memorial services and a solemn mass in honour of him who was born four centuries too soon, the Italian Luther, whose eyes were not to behold the dawn of the Reformation his faith forecast.

VIII

A FOURTEENTH-CENTURY
NEW WOMAN

VIII

A FOURTEENTH-CENTURY
NEW WOMAN

THE Pensione della Santa Caterina, the
quaintest, cleanest, and altogether
most home-like Traveller's Refuge we
have found on the Continent, is our abid-
ing-place during our stay in Siena.

The city itself is a treasury of rich and
rare interests to historian and archæolo-
gist. "They say," and we choose to believe, that it was founded by Senio, the
son of Remus, hunted from Rome by his
uncle Romulus. We receive the legend
into good and credulous hearts, laughing,
once and again, at the perverse inclination
to reverse the outlaw's relationship by
saying "Uncle Remus." The easy belief
is "rubbed in" at every third corner by
the group of the nursing wolf and twin

babies in bronze or stone. We counted ten iron pillars capped by it in one drive through the streets. The streets, that are the steepest we have ever slid down or trudged up; the hoary towers and palace façades fretted to the eaves with carvings a thousand years old; the unbroken wall of ruddy bricks, as old and as hard as the grey stones, belting the eyrie of Longobard kings and Ghibelline, of Guelph and the Dukes of Lorraine,—are replete with fascination.

Yet the name and the fame of a woman drew us to Siena. And staunch Protestants though we are, our first visit in the town is to the Fullonica, otherwise the house of Giacomo Benincasa, the "fullone," or dyer, whose daughter Catherine has given more repute to her native town than all the warriors, artists, and sages who had part in Siena's glory and in her humiliation.

As a matter of course, and as we had expected, superstition has conspired with bad taste to do away with every trace of domestic occupation, such as would have

made the respectable mediæval abode of a
respectable tradesman a source of reverential delight to the intelligent pilgrim.
When we have gained the head of the
flight of stone steps, glossy with age, leading from the street to the door of the
house, and which were here in Catherine's
lifetime, disillusion begins its foul work.
The roof, under which twenty-five children
were born to Giacomo and Lapa, his wife
(who, by the way, lived to the age of
ninety), has given place to the arches and
loftier ceilings of a chapel. The *loggia*
and a church are built over the garden
where the fourteen children who grew to
man's and woman's estate played and
quarrelled and made up again, and Catherine tended the flowers she loved always
and wove into garlands on saints' days,
and bound into bouquets for her sick pen-
sioners. The room where she collected
her co-workers of the order of the Mantellata to help her sew for the town poor is
deformed into a gaudy oratory ; in the
floor of her tiny bedroom we are invited
to look at the stone pillow on which she

laid her head at night after a day of toil, fastings, and prayers. The stone is protected by a grating from the hands and lips of pitying visitors. A glass frame contains fragments of her veils; the head and upper part of her walking-stick; the vinaigrette she used in the wards of pest-houses, and to revive the plague-stricken creatures who fell dying in the streets; the lantern that lighted her steps when summoned by night on errands of mercy; and, what drives us out of the house in a fit of disgustful impatience, the "*Borsa ove la portata da Roma da Siena la sacra testa della Santa,*"—the bag in which the head of the saint was brought from Rome to Siena.

She died at the early age of thirty-three. The next year, "the Republic of Siena having expressed by a deputation of its citizens to the Roman Pontiff its jealousy of the honour of the possession of the body of the saint," the Pope (Urban VI.) ordered the "pious mutilation," and presented the head to Catherine's native town.

A peep into Giacomo's workshop is a

ENTRANCE TO SAINT CATHERINE'S HOUSE.

welcome diversion of unpleasing thoughts. It adjoins the chapel that was his dwelling, and opens into the salesroom where his wares were exposed for sale. Upon shelves running around three sides of the room are queer little parcels, all of the same size, and bearing a surprising resemblance to neat paint-pots. Each is gayly coloured, and emblazoned with the arms of the noble families whose representatives have visited the place and left tokens of reverential esteem for dyer and daughter.

Hurrying out to avert the profanation of a genuine, nineteenth-century laugh, we are arrested upon the stone stair by what brings back the tone of thought and speech we have wished to maintain throughout what is, in effect, a pious pilgrimage.

High up on the wall of a house across the way is a stone label bearing the figure of a goose in bold relief. We are in the Ward of the Goose *(Contrada d'Oca)*, a district peopled in 1337, the year of Catherine Benincasa's birth, by artisans, small

shopkeepers, and day-labourers.   In the
thirty-three years that followed, it became
the most illustrious quarter of the city, although still tenanted by the lower classes,
and only because it was the lowly born
woman's home.

The strait, precipitous street is more
like a tunnel than a thoroughfare, and
the prospect of the distant country is seen
at the other end of the vista as in a massive frame.   Hills—noble in outline, soft
and rich in colour, with silver-grey swath-
ings of olive orchards drawn across their
breasts—meet the unfathomable blue of
the Italian firmament.   At the foot of the
street is the famous Fonte Branda, built
in the twelfth century.   Lion's heads, fe-
rocious through all these centuries, are
thrust out from the wall, and within the
arched enclosure is a series of square
tanks, the upper emptying into the lower.
Here, ever since the lions took up their
watch and ward above, the Sienese women
have washed household linen, and scolded,
and held a Gossips' Exchange, as they are
doing this very hour.   The clear water of

the upper tank becomes yeasty with suds in the second and third.   The soiled linen is dipped into the pool common to all who come, drawn back to the marble edge of the tank, soaped abundantly, scrubbed with a stiff brush, swashed about in the water, again drawn up, wrung, and tossed into baskets.   The din of slapping the wet clothes upon the marble ledge, sousing, rubbing, and shaking them, is a staccato accompaniment to the shrill clack of un-modulated peasant voices.   The foot-path winding up the cliff behind the fountain is the shortest route to the Church of San Dominico, and we begin the ascent, pursued by the tumult, and pausing, midway, for another look at the singular scene.

Six hundred years ago the women of the *Contrada d'Oca* were working, quarrelling, and hobnobbing noisily together, when the dyer's daughter, — eyed with affectionate reverence by the many, with idle curiosity by some, by a very few enviously, —stayed her feet on the way to the place of prayer, to ask gently after this one's young child, and to offer her services in

9

nursing that one's agèd mother, or to take home the family mending of the over-wrought mother of a large family. She never volunteered censure, or adverse criticism in the hearing of others than the sinner's self ; as a child-saint, whose visions and aspirations set her apart from the rest of Giacomo and Lapa's brood, she was never priggish. Humility grew and mel-lowed into meekness with her years. We can think how the clamour—louder than the sparrings and cacklings of a poultry-yard, and not unlike them in emulous dis-cords—if hushed while Catherine talked with the workers, swelled out anew as the slight form disappeared over the brow of the bank. The foot-path is lined now, and doubtless was then, with the drying "wash," spread upon bushes and turf. One wizened little crone toils up ahead of us with a basket of damp linen, as big, and apparently as heavy, as herself, on her back. A pair of the superb white oxen of the Siena *campagna*, harnessed to a cart, bar-ricades the direct route, and she will not diverge by so much as a foot from the

beaten path.   In a voice as shrill and cross
as a guinea-hen's, she calls the owner from
his house, "to take his beasts out of an
honest woman's road," and when he obeys,
goes on upward, grumbling at every step.

Such were Catherine of Siena's social
compeers and daily associates.   Soul and
thought might soar into celestial ether ; her
feet were bound to coarsest mire.   We
picture to ourselves the fragile figure,
quickening its speed involuntarily to gain
the holy silence of the ugly church and
escape from the windy storm of tempers,
the tempest of tongues.

There is a high mass in San Dominico
to-day.   We are met at the entrance by
the smell of incense, the sound of chanting
voices, the sight of a kneeling crowd as-
sembled just without a small but ornate
chapel dedicated to St. Catherine.   It is
lined with exquisite paintings.   A fresco
by Sodoma, representing the saint's ecstatic
swoon in the arms of two attendant nuns,
is startling in beautiful realism as seen in
the subdued light shed by the altar-lamps.
We have happened upon a "holy day,"

we speedily discover, and one of the half-dozen or so a year when the head of St. Catherine is exhibited alike to the believing and the skeptical.   We see it—a livid *memento mori*, enough like her portraits to pain, as well as repel, us.   It is enclosed in a hermetically sealed tabernacle, but the flare of the altar-candles falls full upon it. Some of the women weep, all kneel and cross themselves, eyes bent upon the holy relic ceded to Siena by the gracious See of Rome.

After one swift look, we turn away and retreat noiselessly from the crowd, finding our way, without guide or sacristan, to what we came hither to see,—the real chapel and oratory of Catherine of Siena.

Such a plain, bare room to eyes aching from the gorgeousness of the shrine built over and above the poor, dismembered head ! A few cheap frescoes ; a mean altar at one end ; above the altar the one authentic likeness of Catherine extant, painted by an artist who was her disciple and dear friend ; a tablet or two, and stone benches built into the walls—these are all

SAINT CATHERINE OF SIENA.

The only authentic portrait extant.

we see, and we are thankful. Thankful, especially, that besides ourselves, not a human creature enters the room during the silent, busy half-hour we spend in the effort to winnow biography from tradition, and history from ecclesiastical and *ex cathedra* detail.

For we do not forget in Protestant and rational intolerance with the usual run of the " Lives of the Saints," that Catherine Benincasa was no more a myth than Joan of Arc, or than Bernardino Ochino, born, like her, in the Ward of the Goose, whose " words," said the Emperor Charles V., " would move stones to tears." The fourteenth century produced no woman who was her equal, few men who excelled her in mental gifts, and none who were her superiors in virtue. We have read, and then turned our backs upon, the entablatured inscription telling that " Here she was invested with the habit of St. Dominic ; and she was the first woman who ever wore it. Here, she remained withdrawn from the world, listening to the Divine Services of the Church, and here,

continually in divine colloquy, she con-
versed familiarly with Jesus Christ, her
Spouse.   Here, leaning against this pilas-
ter, she was rapt in frequent ecstasies."

The tales of her trances; her miracles
of faith, of healing and of prophecy; the
visions and revelations in which she believed as devoutly as the Maid of Orleans
in her " Voices "—are to be interpreted
by the help of latter-day common-sense,
and appreciation of intellectual and spirit-
ual laws unknown in the Middle Ages.
We are sure that Catherine was sincere in
her mysticism, not upon the authority of
the forty biographies written of her, but
because she was a good and a truthful
woman.   We know—thanks to the abundant enlightenment of these same latter
days—that the asceticism which ruined
her health and brought her to an early
grave, the hair-cloth, and the starvation of
her beautiful body, the stone pillow and
the bed of planks, surrounded by other
planks, that she might ever be mindful of
death and the coffin,—were grievous er-
rors, even in a generation that accounted

them unto its holy ones as righteousness.
Setting all this aside, the wonder of her
day is even more a wonder unto ours.

Born a year before the outbreak of the
plague that reduced the population of Siena from one hundred thousand to one-
fifth of that number, she lived in childhood
and early womanhood under the chill
shadow of that awful visitation. The
brevity of human life and the vanity of
mortal hopes ; the supreme importance of
preparation for Eternity, and the duty
of each pious soul to other souls,—were
borne in upon her young mind by all that
she saw and heard until she resolved to
think of nothing but Christ and His kingdom, to devote every power of her mind,
every hour of her time, every affection of
her soul, to His service. In the exalta-
tion induced by resolve and effort, she
beheld, when but six years of age, "looking up to the glorious clouds of evening
over the gable end of the church of S.
Dominico, a vision of Jesus, very gloriously
apparelled, and terrible in majesty and
beauty, Who looked towards her and

smiled lovingly upon her, extending His hand in blessing."

When the trance was rudely broken by her little brother's tug upon her hand, she "turned homewards, weeping. From this moment she became more grave and thoughtful than before."

To the like seasons of rapt devotion, when she could not have told whether she were in the body or out of it, may be referred her mystic espousal to Christ, a claim made for, rather than by, her, that has prejudiced the minds of sober Protestants against her whole character and professions.

Again translating into our everyday speech the pious hyperbolism of her times, we draw from the tale of St. Catherine's Marriage the simple truth that hers was a "life hid with Christ in God." Rowland Hill, the great English preacher, clothed the same longing and its glorious fulfilment in the homely hymn he loved to chant, walking up and down his room while his face "was as the face of an angel":

"But this I do find,
We two are so joined,
He 'll not go to glory and leave me behind."

We do not misunderstand St. Paul's talk of " bearing about in his body the marks of the Lord Jesus." When Catherine Benincasa used a similar figure of her wasted and racked frame, her admirers, unlearnèd, and full of superstitious fancies, whispered, awe-stricken, stories of the "*stigmata*," and churchly annals have aided church-ridden artists in the perpetuation of the legend. Catherine's biographers, contemporary and of later date, expressly say that she never spoke of having received the *stigmata*.

With all her dreams and mystic revelations, her religion was practical and most Christlike. She was full of good works and alms-deeds which she did, esteeming no office menial, no gift a sacrifice that lessened the sufferings, or heightened the happiness of Christ's " little ones." She was always cheerful, even joyous, we are told, full of tenderest charity for the erring, yet courageous in rebuking wilful sins. At the age of sixteen, she was the leader of the order of the Mantellata, a Woman's Charitable Society, as we would term it. In 1374 the plague broke out again in Siena. The rich and great fled from the city ; those who could not go died by the thousand. "Sometimes the priests and those who carried out the dead sat down to rest, and never rose again," and some of the poorer streets were literally blocked with corpses. At the head of her Mantellatas, Catherine wrought, night and day, "in the most infected quarters," nursing the sick, feeding the starving, preparing the dead for burial. Instances are not wanting of what were rated as miraculous cures wrought by her prayers, and here, again, the testimony of her disciples outran her modest confession of means and end. She believed firmly, she said, that "the prayer of faith shall save the sick, in every case in which that fulfilment was for the good of the sufferer, and for the glory of God."

As who of us who calls himself a Christian does not ?

Furthermore, she " persuaded the patient to make a confession of sin, then spoke peace to his conscience through faith in Jesus Christ, and sought to inspire him with a joyous courage and resolution." No wiser regimen could have been carried on in the plague-smitten city when men's hearts were failing them for fear, the fear that slew more than the pestilence.

She visited hardened criminals in their prisons, going, fearlessly and alone, to talk and pray with the most depraved of these ; attended them to the scaffold and received their dying testimony to the saving Faith she held and taught.

But the circumstance that set her apart in a peculiar sense from others of her age and sex at a time when marriage or the cloister was the only choice granted to women of every degree, was that the Dominican Fathers, acceding to her cherished desire to preach the Gospel of Christ, actually commissioned her to act as an Evangelist, and that public opinion sustained her in the New Departure. She maintained that her warrant for the bold innovation upon established customs, and defiance of conventional prejudices, came from a Higher Power than the ghostly Fathers who had received her into the third order of the Dominicans. I quote from her answer to the Divine "leading" sent in answer to her prayers :

"Lord! not my will, but Thine, be done! for I am only darkness and Thou art all light. . . . How can I, who am so miserable and fragile, be useful to my fellow-creatures? My sex is an obstacle, as Thou, Lord, knowest, as well because it is contemptible in men's eyes, as because propriety forbids me any freedom of converse with the other sex."

The struggle closed with her humble— "*Behold the handmaiden of the Lord. Be it unto me even as Thou wilt !*"

In one of her many itineraries she addressed an audience of two thousand people, "beseeching them, for the love of Jesus, to be at peace with one another, and to follow the banner of the Prince of Peace."

"Peace" was the word ever upon her

lips in that turbulent age. She reconciled private citizens, families, religious fraternities, and political parties. She was sent for to Florence, where she was the guest of the Soderini family ; to Pisa, and was met on the way by a wealthy merchant with a " goodly company " of leading men to conduct her and her friends to the merchant's palace. From this place she wrote " many letters on the affairs of the Church and the Republics," and there conceived, and began to communicate to prelate and soldier, the idea of the union of all Christendom in a Crusade for the recovery of Jerusalem from the hands of the Turks.

Her most notable achievement was the successful embassy, undertaken " at the Divine command," to Pope Gregory XI. at Avignon, the then Papal Court. Against his own will, and in the teeth of fierce opposition from the most influential party at Court, this delicate woman of the people wrought upon him, by argument and pleadings, to restore the See to Rome, and it became once more the seat of

government.   As an example of her manner of dealing with the Pontiff I give a
brief extract from her first letter to him :

"You will never reduce your subjects
to submission by the sword.   .   .   .   The
spirit of strife and the absence of virtue,
these are the two things which are causing
the Church to lose ground more and more.
If you wish to regain what you have lost,
your only means of doing so is to re-
trace your steps, and to reconquer your
lost dominions by the encouragement of
virtue and by peace.   Pardon, beloved
Father, my presumptuous boldness."

A Roman Catholic writer says : " She
struck at the root of the evil,—the im-
morality of the clergy and the odious
government of the Papal legates."

In another letter she firmly and frankly
reminds the Pope that his prelates and
priests "are a thousand times more en-
tangled in the luxury and vanities of the
world than the laity ; for indeed, many of
the laity put the pastors to shame by their
pure and holy lives.   .   .   .   Open your
eyes, O Father, and see what these people

are who are called apostles of the flock, and how they devour the poor; how their souls are filled with greed and hatred, and how they have made their bodies vessels of every kind of abomination."

It is not easy in reading this and other of her letters to credit that she taught herself to write after she was eighteen years of age. Simple as an unspoiled child, when she was the most famous woman in all Italy, she liked best to be known as "The Daughter of the Republic" and "The Child of the People." Other and loving epithets were showered upon her by her townsmen. She was "Our Lady of the Contrada d'Oca," "The People's Catherine," "The Blessed Plebeian." Her *Meditations* and her *Philosophy*, like her epistles, are clear in diction, strong, and even eloquent in style, and full of the pure and lofty spirit she carried, like a charméd treasure, in a violent, besotted, and licentious age.

She died April 29, 1380, in Rome, spent by the heroic effort to infuse purity and true faith into a corrupt Church.

"Lord! Thou callest me, and I go to Thee! Not on account of my merits, but solely on account of Thy mercy!" were among her last words.

The list of her correspondents is a curious study. Among them were Florentine jailors; Sienese prisoners; "an abominably profligate man, name not mentioned"; a Jew usurer of immense wealth; John Hawkwood, the English soldier of fortune; her "little niece, Jenny"; Gregory XI. and his successor, Urban VI.; Bernabos Visconti, the tyrant Duke of Milan; a currier and his wife at Lucca; Laurencio di Pino, Professor of Law in the University of Bologna; the Signoria of Siena,—etc., etc., the roll embracing every rank in society and half-a-dozen nationalities.

She "had most of her visions" in this neglected chapel, unadorned to-day save by such memories as we have conjured up. She kneaded bread for the public poor with her own hands and baked it in the big, yawning oven we saw, this morning, in the disused cellar of the Pensione di Santa Caterina.

One of her sayings was, " Patience—the touchstone of all the virtues."   The sweet saint and true woman, the counsellor of princes, the confidante of weavers' wives, —the uncomplaining invalid who made of the pangs she belittled smilingly as "gentle pains," so many rounds in the ladder by which she neared the loftiest type of Christian life,—had proved the virtue of her touchstone.

10

IX

THE GINEVRA TALE

IX

THE GINEVRA TALE

"THERE is no story so perfect as the Ginevra Tale."

Thus one, who, when we have made allowance for inaccuracies, extravagance of sentiment, and a floridness of style that is often tawdry, gives us the very breath and soul and light of Florence.

As a novel *Pascarel* is below criticism; historically, it is full of flaws. As a prose poem, it brings us, wherever we may be in body, face to face, heart to heart, with the glorious mistress of the Arno, and

"With dreamful eyes,
The spirit lies,—"

not "under the walls of Paradise," but dwells within the dear old streets, cool with purple shadows in the hottest noontide, and, morning, noon, and midnight,

thronged with ghosts that are never laid.
I asked for the "perfect story" this
afternoon in a bookseller's shop, not a
hundred paces away from the Street of
the Dead (*Via della Morte*) changed from
the *Via del Campanile* because of what
happened here, one night, in a Past that
is grey, but never decrepit. Scribe has
told it to us in a poem made almost trite
by average and amateur elocutionists.
Italian ballad-mongers count the versified
tale as a stock article, and it has been
put upon the stage in yet another, and
more meretricious, form. But there is no
printed authentic version of the romance
in detail. We have to go back to Boccaccio for the graphic outline of an event
which, for thrilling dramatic interest, casts
every other Florentine legend into the
shade. Boccaccio availed himself of it,
but did not invent it.

"But, yes, it is quite true. It is history, not tradition," said the bookseller,
surprised at our questioning. "She was
Ginevra degli Amieri. You will see from
that corner,"—pointing through his door,

—"the site of her husband's house in the *Corso degli Adimari.*"

Instead of obeying the direction of his finger, we have come to the Square of the Duomo, and, recalling the fact that the door of the family vault in which the supposed corpse was interred, was between Cathedral and Campanile, we locate the same to our satisfaction. "The lily of Florence, blossoming in stone," the Campanile of Giotto, "the model and mirror of perfect architecture," was then unfinished, a truncated shaft, and but a mass of gloom in the darkness of the night, when the affrighted creature struggled back to life. All about the base of the great Cathedral were tombs, and the Piazza was paved with lettered slabs, shut down fast upon burial-vaults. The resting-places of their dead were but carelessly guarded by their rich citizens who had the right to lay their kindred here. The tomb of the Medici in the Church of San Lorenzo, for four centuries, had no securer protection from grave-robbers than wooden doors and common bolts and hasps.

Ginevra Amieri, in love with one man, was married to another by the will of her patrician father. " He preferred Francesco Agolanti to Antonio Rondinelli, because he "—Agolanti—" was of noble family," says Boccaccio. Also, that Ginevra " could never be reconciled to the marriage that was arranged for her." She had been the wife of Agolanti several years, when she fell ill, and, sinking into a sort of cataleptic trance, was pronounced dead by the physicians. The hasty interment customary at that day in Italy took place within twenty-four hours ; the stone was lowered to its place over the mouth of the crypt, and the mourners went their ways to their homes.

It was midnight when Ginevra awoke. She lay in an open niche, dressed in grave-clothes ; her wrists were bound firmly in the form of a cross upon her breast, and she knew the stifling blackness of the place to be that of the charnel-house. As soon as the horror of the truth let her use her senses, she untied the ribbon from her wrists, groped her way to the steps lead-

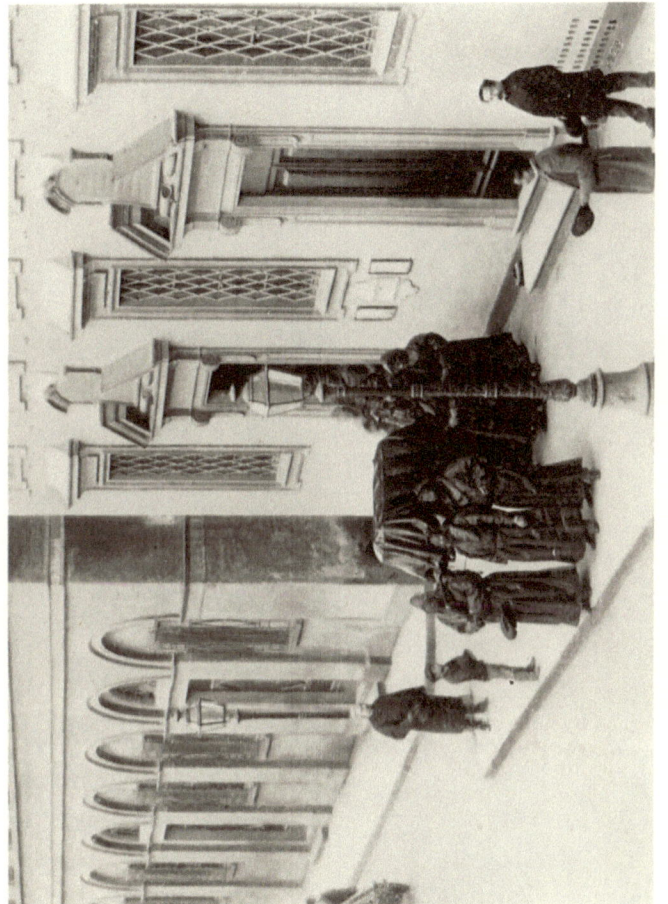

HEADQUARTERS OF THE MISERICORDIA IN FLORENCE.

ing to the upper world, and exerted all her
strength to raise the stone laid over the
entrance to the vault, succeeding finally
in sliding it far enough aside to allow the
passage of her body.   Her only garment
was her shroud ; her feet were bare.   Putting out her hands in the obscurity, she
could feel on one side the cold stones of
the Cathedral, on the other the marbles
of the Campanile, and guided her course
by these into the unlighted streets.   Still
feeling her way past the headquarters of
the Misericordia,—and, we may hope,
gleaning courage from the thought of the
love and mercy of man to his suffering
fellows, typified by the Order,—she entered the narrow way that now commem-
orates her sorrowful wanderings, and
emerged into the street on which stood
her home.

The husband, who believed himself a
widower, was sleeping—we charitably suppose—"for sorrow."   Awakened by the
irregular knocking upon the lower door,
he looked from the window and asked
who was there.   A feeble voice answered

with his wife's name.   In the disorder of
wits produced by the abrupt awakening
and the shock of the supernatural visitation, he cast one glance below, and seeing the glimmer of white garments, cried
out to the spirit to begone, shut the
casement in deadly terror, and fell to
saying his prayers, lest wood and stone
might not avail to exclude the bodiless
intruder.

Her father lived in the Mercato Vecchio.
That most picturesque antique of Florence has been demolished and swept away
by the besom of Sanitary Reform. We are
not at a loss, however, as to the site of
the Amieri house. It was so near the
Church of S. Andrea that the terrified
parent might have bethought himself of
the comparative security from diabolical
intrusions afforded by the vicinity of the
sanctuary.   But one look from his iron-
grated lattice at the shivering Thing that
cried to him in Ginevra's voice to let her
in, drove every thought from his mind except the frantic desire to exorcise the lying
devil, or ghost. He shrieked to her to go

MERCATO VECCHIO (NOW DEMOLISHED).

"That most picturesque antique of Florence."

away, and bolted his window against her sobs and entreaties.

We return upon the imaginary trail left by her bleeding feet over the rough stones, to the *Via Calzaioli*, now one of the noisiest of the narrow throats of Florentine traffic,—on that night as still as the tomb the deserted woman had left, and wellnigh as gloomy, a deep well, between lofty houses whose projecting eaves almost met above her head.

In the porch of S. Bartolommeo, an old church even then, she laid her down, chilled to the bone and heart, spent and despairing, and prayed for death, as, a little while before, she had prayed for strength to hold the life given back to her.

"Then," says the simple story, "she remembered her beloved Rondinelli, who had always proved faithful to her."

Remembered him! What woman who lives and has ever loved and been loved, will believe that she had forgotten him for one instant after she knew that she was still in the same world with him? I have, never-

theless, always been glad, in my secret
soul, that Ginevra went, first of all, to the
husband whose she was by the law of
the land, her Church, and her conscience. Dizzied though she was by illness and fright, the faintness of dying
and the shock of coming back to life, her
instinct of honour and right held fast.
Her solemn vows had been plighted to
Francesco Agolanti, and death had not,
after all, parted them. Where he was,
was home, and to that asylum she sped,
with never a thought of seeking any
other.

One variation of the tale sends her to
the house of an uncle, after her father had
driven her from his door. This kinsman
lived in the Mercato Vecchio, not far from
the home of her girlhood. He, too, had
repulsed her with horror and loathing,
before she crawled, like a shot dove, into
the church-porch to die.

We are gratified by the circumstance
that the street into which we next direct
our steps still bears the name of Rondinelli. Since his was not a noble house,

and therefore low-esteemèd in the eyes of haughty Bernardo Amieri, it is hardly likely, or so we reason, that the thoroughfare was called after his forefathers. We choose to synchronise the re-christening with that of the *Via del Campanile*—from that night and forevermore, the *Via della Morte*—and make the change one of the scores of memorials to faithful love and heroic endeavour the ancient Florentines delighted to honour, and to bequeath to prosaic generations following.

The actual abode of Antonio Rondinelli was razed to the ground centuries ago. We do not require the help of stone walls and barred windows and the heavy lower door against which the fainting woman sank, after one feeble knock upon the panels, in our reproduction of the scene. Antonio did not sleep that night. At last, after years of hopeless separation, his love was again all his, in the spirit that had never truly belonged to Agolanti. He might dream and think of her now, without sin. Without so much as a thought of wrong, her freed soul might

commune with his. Through all the
years of the Eternity in which he would,
one day, rejoin her, they would live and
love together. Aroused by the low rap-
ping at his door from musings sweet and
welcome as visions from that Blessèd
Land—so much the more blessèd because
of her dwelling therein—he called to the
unseen visitor :

"Who is there?"

"It is I—Ginevra!"

It was scarcely a surprise. That she
should speak to him was as natural as her
coming to him in the beautiful dreams that
had held his eyes waking.

There is a book-mark in our worn copy
of *Pascarel.* We open at that page and
read, leaning against the wall of Rondinelli's house. The beat of passing feet
upon the sidewalk, the roar of wheels and
click of hoofs, gay shop-windows and cas-
ual and curious glances,—are the dream.
The cold night, the form at the open casement bending to listen to the faint accents
from below, the drooping figure, prone
on the earth, vague and dim, as if her

empty shroud had been tossed into the deep embrasure of the doorway,—these are the real things with which we have to do.

We do not read aloud. Yet the air stirs and throbs with words we hear, rather than see :

"Then, at last, the lover's threshold, the timid summons of despair, the open door, the instant welcome ; not a doubt, not a question, not a fear. Living or dead, of heaven or of hell—what matter which ?

"What matter whence she came ?

"What matter what she brought ?

"Welcome, thrice welcome, as flowers in the May-time.

". . . And it was all true, too, here, in this *Via della Morte*."

"His parents," we have read elsewhere, "cared for her tenderly, and she was soon restored to health."

The mother, from whom the son got his faithful heart, is the actor that completes the group for us. Her gentle hands were busy with the wanderer, no longer homeless, when she awoke from her

swoon; in her safe and honourable keeping her son's love remained until she became his wife.

Scribe, and Italian "Walks" and " Saun-
terings," bring us down from the supreme
height of sympathetic interest by going
into the minutiæ of the solemn absurdity
of the decision arrived at by Church
Courts. To wit: that Madonna Ginevra
Agolanti, having died officially, and been
interred in good and regular order, eccle-
siastically, was now *not*, henceforth, and
for all time. Furthermore, that the mar-
riage-contract between her and Messer
Francesco Agolanti was legally dissolved
by her decease, and hereafter not binding
upon either party. This decreed, it was
no concern of the solemn owl, the State
Church, what happened to either of them,
thereafter. Messer Francesco was free to
take unto himself another wife, and neither
the Holy Father of Rome nor the Signoria
of the Florentine Republic had jurisdic-
tion over a ghost.

To us, the Perfect Tale is rounded to a
faultless close with the opening of that

door; the lifting of the helpless woman from the threshold of Antonio Rondinelli's door, in his strong arms, and to his faithful bosom.

"And it was all true, too, here, in this *Via della Morte!*"

X

JOHN KEATS IN ROME

X

JOHN KEATS IN ROME

THE Spanish Steps are as well known
to the tourist in Rome as St. Peter's
Church. At the top of the stately flight
is the Church of San Trinità del Monte,
her twin towers rising light and strong
against the sky. At the foot is the Fon-
tana della Barca, a landmark of great and
uncertain age. The gentle babble of the
playing waters, unheard a dozen paces
away when the fashionable din of the Piazza di Spagna is at its loudest, is distinct
to the nocturnal lounger upon the upper-
most landing of the stone stairway.

It rises in broken, musical whispers to
the open window of a second-story front
room of "the first house on the right, as
you ascend the steps of the Trinità del
Monte."

This was Joseph Severn's description of the lodgings hired for himself and his invalid friend John Keats, by an English physician resident in Rome.   The two young men arrived in Rome in mid-November, 1820.   After the first week of December Keats never quitted this chamber.   "An accursed lodging-place," Severn calls it when he had to spend his last crown to save his dying companion from ejectment into the street.   "If he dies," he adds, "all the beds and furniture will be burnt and the walls scraped, and they will come on me for a hundred crowns or more."

Again, he inveighs savagely against "this comfortless Italy, this wilderness of a place for an invalid."

The lodging-place is not comfortless as we see it.   The room is clean, spacious and well furnished, one of a suite occupied by a highly respectable family.   The location is airy and central, and far more expensive now than when it was let to the two *forestieri*, seventy-eight winters ago. It is, nevertheless, easy to picture it as dismally unhomelike and inadequate to the

necessities of tenants accustomed to the
comforts of their native England.   Decent
furniture, fire, and food both dainty and
nutritious, were to be had in the Italy of
that date for money, and there were enough
English residents in the Eternal City to
make up a pleasant circle for themselves.
Keats had come to Rome, " his last place
of torture and of rest," upon borrowed
money.   Severn, an artist of promise,—
abundantly fulfilled in after-life—had received a gold medal for a picture exhibited in the Royal Academy, and, with it,
an honorarium in value sufficient to de-
fray the costs of three years' study in Italy.
To the Circle aforesaid they were utterly
unknown.   Besides their physician and his
kind wife, who sent broths and jellies to
her husband's patient, they had few acquaintances, and apparently no active
friends in the city.

The comrades had been friends for seven
years, and, since the setting-in of Keats's
mortal malady, intimates.   Severn's admiration of Keats as the embodiment of
the artist's " complete idea of a poet," and

genuine fondness for the ardent, wayward
genius, were deepened by a peculiar element of tenderness in the nature of the
stalwart elder of the twain—a yearning
over hurt and helpless things, which drew
out his whole soul in pity for the unhappy
boy. For, Keats, small of stature and
delicate of feature, with glorious eyes that
filled with tears, and sensitive lips that
trembled like a child's, at a sudden rush
of thought or emotion, although but two
years Severn's junior, looked, at twenty-
five, a mere lad beside him.

During the two months passed by them
in this chamber, the duties of the devoted
attendant were manifold and incongruous.
But for the cheerful heroism of his affection for the object of these cares, they
would have irked him past endurance.
He had hoped to send another picture to
the Academy this winter, and to push forward vigorously the studies he had come
to Rome to prosecute. His easel leaned
idly against the wall ; palette, brushes and
paints were not unpacked. He was Keats's
nurse by day and his sole watcher by night.

Rising in the raw dawn of wintry morn-
ings, he kindled the fire and always prepared his friend's breakfast with his own.
Sometimes he cooked all their meals after
buying the materials for the same ; he
made beds, and swept the stone floor ;
"sat by the bedside and read all day, and
at night humoured him in all his wanderings," his heart aching with loving compassion that left no room for complaint
of his own disappointment and privations.

When the sick man, frenzied by fever
and nervous irritability, leaped out of bed,
declaring, "This day *shall* be my last!"
the guardian gathered him in his strong
arms, as he might lift a fretful baby, and
laid him upon the pillows, wiped the bright
blood from the poor, white lips, and petted
and soothed him into comparative quiet.

On February 14, Severn wrote to Mrs.
Brawne of the "great quietness and peace"
that had succeeded the fearful unrest of
many weeks.

"It seems like a delightful sleep to me.
*I have been tossing about in the tempest of
his mind for so long!*"

The simple phrase holds a volume of meaning, a depth and completeness of unselfish sympathy, such as is given to few men to inspire, or to feel.

The sovereign commonwealth of readers and the oligarchy of reviewers have, since then, done full credit to the genius of John Keats.   From the day he left his cradle to that in which Joseph Severn laid to rest in a foreign land the shattered frame from which the lungs had wasted entirely away, two months earlier, he had never a sane mind in a sane body.   His biographers throw away time in disputing whether or not Byron wrote the truth in declaring that the poet's life was " snuffed out by an article."   His brother's summing up of the lamentable case covered more and tenable ground :

" *Blackwood* and *The Quarterly*, associated with our family disease, consumption, were ministers of death sufficiently venomous, cruel, and deadly to have consigned one of less sensibility to a premature grave."

The seeds of death were implanted in

GRAVES OF KEATS AND SEVERN IN THE PROTESTANT CEMETERY IN ROME.

his constitution by his mother. From her
he drew, also, his sensuous temperament,
his intolerance of pain and the capacity
for loving and suffering with fierce unrea-
son that hurried on the inevitable end.
" The horrid morbidity" he deplores in a
rational hour, finally ate into and con-
sumed his heart.   How much of this was
due to ill-health, how much to "venomous " critics, and how little to natural lack
of balance and to undisciplined passion, is
a nice question which, it seems to us, is
best settled by his latest biographer, William Michael Rossetti.   His *Life of Keats*
is our pocket companion in the silent upper chamber where torture ceased, and
rest began.

Fanny Brawne was a poor creature upon
which to stake love and life, and Keats
knew this to be true in the lucid intervals
of his infatuation.   Rossetti gives the key
to the wretched entanglement in two judicial lines :

" He was in a state of feeling propense
to love. *Some* woman was required to fill
the void in his heart."

For a while after her image was pro-
jected upon the sensitised surface, he could
play with it coolly. In a letter to his
brother, he catalogues certain physical
traits of Miss Brawne's, as " good," others,
"tolerable," one or two as "bad-ish."
"She wants sentiment in every feature ";
as to mind, she is " ignorant," in deportment, "monstrous," and "a minx." Almost
as soon as this letter could reach Louis-
ville, Kentucky, where the George Keatses
lived, the lover swears to his frivolous
divinity :—" From the very first week I
knew you I wrote myself your vassal," and
"all I can bring you is a swooning admiration of your beauty."

Naturally suspicious, and made more
misanthropic by the hidden fires of his
disease, he never trusted her for a single
hour. He had read her too well, and re-
collected too faithfully the many evidences
she had given him of lightness of mind
and greed of admiration. After sickness
made him prisoner and kept him absent
from her, he was " torn by ideas of her
volatility, and fickleness," and hated, while

he hugged, his chains. Her flirtations
with Charles Armitage Brown, of whom
Keats writes at this very time—" I know
his love and friendship for me "—drove
him to coarseness of accusation. " I see
nothing but thorns for the future," says
the last letter penned to Fanny before his
journey southward. " Wherever I may
be next winter, in Italy—*or nowhere*—
Brown will be living near you with his
indecencies. I see no prospect of any rest.
Suppose me in Rome. I should there
see you, as in a magic glass, going to and
from town at all hours——

" I wish I could infuse a little confidence
of human nature into my heart. I cannot
muster any. The world is too brutal for
me. I am glad there is such a thing as
the grave! I am sure I shall never have
any rest till I get there. . . .

" I wish I was either in your arms, full
of faith, or that a thunderbolt would strike
me dead!"

If anything could heighten the profound
pity, and the regret that nearly trenches
upon repulsion with which we read these

ravings, it would be another letter, addressed by the lover when actually *en voyage*, to the man of whose " indecencies " he had complained to his betrothed.

" I think "—run the sentences dictated by the calm sorrow of his then mood—"for my sake, you would be a friend to Miss Brawne when I am dead. You think she has many faults. For my sake think she has not one. It there is anything you can do for her by word or deed, I know you will do it. .   .   .

" The thought of leaving Miss Brawne is beyond everything horrible—the sense of darkness coming over me—I eternally see her figure, eternally vanishing. Some of the phrases she was in the habit of using during my last nursing in Wentworth Place " (the Brawnes' home in Hampstead) " ring in my ears. Is there another life ? Shall I awake and find all this a dream ? There must be. We cannot be created for this sort of suffering. The receiving this letter is to be one of yours."

A passionate, pessimistic boy, in whom

earthly suffering was never to work out
the Divine purpose, or to yield the peaceable fruits of self-control and charity, he
fought with death as he had fought with
a life that seemed all wrong to his per-
verted perceptions. He would not read
Fanny Brawne's letters when Severn
brought them to his bed.   A glance at the
last that reached him "tore him to pieces."
He charged Severn to see that it was put
into his coffin, with one from his sister;
then countermanded the order, so far as it
related to the letter from his betrothed.

Days of "doubt and horror" dragged
on, and sleepless nights, during which the
horrible suffocation that threatened death
a thousand times before its merciful coming, obliged him to have the windows
open, letting in—as we reflect, with a
a fleeting sense of thankfulness—the plash
and tinkle of the fountain in the square
below, and the call, "Severn,—I am dying!" hastened the faithful watcher to his
side. For the last time the strong arms
lifted him up.

"Don't be frightened! Be firm, and

thank God it has come!" are the words the loving scribe must have recorded with more than gratitude—with sorrowful pride in the rally of whatever was brave and manly in the pitiful wreck that went to pieces upon his constant heart.

So close to our window that we could touch it by leaning over the sill is a tablet, in the outer wall of the house, telling who died here, and when.

"In a room," says a fellow-student with him in the medical college, " Keats was always at the window peering out into space, and it was customary to call the window-seat 'Keats's place.'"

He must have been propped in his chair often, to sit at the casement overlooking the Piazza di Spagna, on the sunny days which, we hope, were many in the winter of 1820–1821. Severn may have brought him into the sunlight in his arms to let him "peer" into the glad, free space without his prison, or at midnight, in the hope of lessening the horrible unrest of fever and asphyxia by a sight of the "patient stars——

Who climb each night the ancient sky."

We pause for a last look at the corner
in which Keats's bed used to stand, then
go silently down the stairs that gave back
the slow echoes of the bearers' tread when
the pitifully light weight of his mortal remains was removed for their long rest.

"I followed his dear body to the grave
on Monday, February 26," wrote Severn
to Fanny Brawne's mother. "The letters
I placed in the coffin with my own
hand."

The order to keep back the last received from Miss Brawne had been re-
voked. Others, also unread, received from
her in previous weeks, went into the coffin
with it, and one from his only sister.

"I long to believe in immortality," he
had told his betrothed, "I shall never be
able to bid you an entire farewell."

And, again—"I wish to believe in immortality! I wish to live with you forever."

We can imagine that the pulseless heart
would quicken with one last painful throb
as the unread letters were laid upon it.

In our thoughtful drive to the Protest-

ant Cemetery, we try to banish the recollection of the story that Miss Brawne could
speak, in after years, flippantly, and with
patronising compassion more dishonouring
to his memory than open ridicule—of
" John Keats, the foolish young poet who
was in love with me."

She was, moreover, not averse to the
measure of distinction that fell to her lot
as the object of this mad folly, after readers and reviewers awoke to the perception
of his glorious gifts, and the loss the world
had sustained when his life flickered out
in discomfort and despair.   Even after her
marriage to another man, she kept Keats's
letters.   She had never understood why
he shrank from talking of their betrothal
to common acquaintances; his resentment
of his friends' "spying upon a secret I
would rather die than share with anybody's
confidence," was silly, and even unkind, in
her estimation.

" Good gods !" he breaks out, fiercely.
" What a shame it is our loves should be
so put into the microscope of a coterie !
Their ' laughs ' should not affect you,

when in competition with one, who, if he never should see you again, would make you the saint of his memory."

From which, and other expressions, we learn that Miss Brawne's associates had twitted her with her lover's proud reticence upon the theme sacred to him, and anything but sacred to her.

" That is arterial blood!   That drop is my death-warrant!" was his verdict at sight of his first hemorrhage.

The same may be said of every word in these *terrible* love-letters.   Each is a drop of life-blood, and their leap from the anguished heart actually appalls us.   No eyes but hers should ever have rested upon the pages.   It was nothing short of vivisection for her to turn them over to public examination and judgment.   And this was done, in effect, by her preservation of them, aware as she was, what use would be made of them when they escaped from her keeping.

We cannot, and we do not care to, forgive her. She outlived her madly-mistaken lover by forty-four years, dying in peaceful respectability, a British matron of years, in 1865.

Long before that, *Endymion, The Pot of Basil,* and *Lamia* took their eternal place among the choicest of English classics, and *The Eve of St. Agnes* was hung in the mental galleries of scholarly critics as the divinest bit of word-painting in the English language. The movement of the poem is a luxury to ear and imagination,—liquid melody,—" a delicate transfusion of sight and emotion into sound," Rossetti says, aptly and eloquently. " *The Eve of St. Agnes* is, *par excellence,* the poem of glamour."

Glamour that holds brain and senses in delicious captivity. The mere repetition of each perfect line is a definite delight ; imagery and description are a chaplet of flawless gems.

" Among the many things he has requested of me to-night this is the principal —that on his grave shall be this—' Here lies one whose name is writ in water,' "—is an entry in the diary Severn sent to Mrs. Brawne.

In obeying the harrowing injunction, the faithful executor prefaced it by a sentence that shows his own hot sympathy with the hounded poet :

" This grave contains all that was mortal of a young English poet, who, on his death-bed, in the bitterness of his heart at the malicious power of his enemies, desired these words to be engraved on his tomb-stone :—'*Here lies one whose name was writ in water.*' February 24, 1821."

It was in a gentler mood, perhaps in the " great quietness and peace " that fell upon him in the last week of his life, like a presage of the everlasting rest, that he whispered one night when Severn thought him asleep,—"*I feel the daisies growing over me !* "

They lift their innocent eyes to ours from his breast, and overrun the turf on all sides. Shelley had seen them before he wrote in the *Adonais* which is an immortal tribute to his dead friend :

" Pass, till the spirit of the spot shall lead
  Thy footsteps to a slope of green access,

Where, like an infant's smile over the dead,
A light of laughing flowers along the grass is
    spread."

It is not possible to pause at this point
in the repetition of the exquisite lines,
when we say them, here and thus :

" And gray walls moulder round on which dull
    Time
Feeds, like a slow fire upon a hoary brand ;
And one keen pyramid, with wedge sublime,
Pavilioning the dust of him who planned
This refuge for his memory, doth stand,
Like flame transformed to marble ; and beneath
A field is spread, on which a newer band
Have pitched in Heaven's smile their camp of
    death,
Welcoming him we love with scarce extinguished
    breath."

Hardy English ivies, lush from the
warmth of southern soil, bind the grave
of Keats to that of his leal, heroic friend,
Joseph Severn, who rejoined him in 1879.

Shelley's heart, plucked, unconsumed,
from his ashes, by Trelawney, after the
cremation at Spezzia, was brought to
Rome and buried in the newer cemetery
of which the city wall is the boundary. Trelawney, his henchman, parasite, and biog-

rapher, was, at his especial and most characteristic request, laid beside Shelley's tomb.

There had been some talk of Keats's wintering with the Shelleys at Pisa, and, after the project was given up, Shelley had still the kindly intention " to be the physician both of his body and of his soul—to keep the one warm, and to teach the other Greek and Spanish."

Violets spread a purple pall over Shelley's heart; rose-thickets, full of bursting buds, cast wavering shadows upon the " *Cor Cordium* " of his memorial-stone.

" It is enough to make one in love with death to think of sleeping in so sweet a spot,"—he had said, with no prevision of what we are looking upon, now.

" The weariness, the fever and the fret,
    Here, where men sit and hear each other groan,
    Where palsy shakes a few sad, last gray hairs,
    Where youth grows pale and spectre-dim, and
        dies—[1]

—are over, and forever, for them both, thank God! and in the world that sets this right.

[1]Keats's *Ode to a Nightingale.*

SHELLEY'S TOMB IN THE PROTESTANT CEMETERY, ROME.

XII.

TOLD ON THE LAGOON.

XI.

TOLD ON THE LAGOON.

A SMALL steamer runs—or creeps—
to Torcello three times a week. It
churns up the stagnant water of the
shallow inlets, thrust like sickly fingers
into the salt marshes of the lonely island,
and is moored against the blackish rocks
abutting what was once a broad and busy
square. It is now a meadow, dotted, in
the springtime, with the white starry
flower we call, in our home across the sea,
the "Star-of-Bethlehem."

Beyond the meadow is a group of buildings, partly in ruins. The little church
dedicated to Santa Fosca, was built more
than twelve hundred years ago, by the
fugitives from Altinum, after the burning
of their town by the Lombards. Landing
upon the island of Torcello, they founded

there a veritable city of refuge. To the
same date belongs the Campanile which
first catches the eyes strained across the
lagoon for a sight of the clustered ruins
and the Cathedral, post-dating them by
two centuries.

The pivotal point of the story to which
we listen in our seven-mile voyage, is this
Cathedral, erected—as nearly as can be
estimated, by consulting the confused
chronological tables of those early days—
about 1040. The foundations were laid
in those of an earlier church, the work of
the Altinese.

Shrinking from the prospect of seeing
Torcello—"*sui generis* for simplicity and
solitude"—in company with a horde of
chattering "trippers," we have hired a
gondola to take us thither. The lagoon
just breathes, and in slow, leisurely heav-
ings, under the clear gray heavens re-
flected in its bosom. There is no glare,
and the gentle stir of the air saves the day
from sultriness ; there is not another gondola within speaking distance. Behind us
is Venice, gradually losing outline and col-

THE "CATHEDRAL GROUP" OF TORCELLO.

our in blending with the pearl-gray horizon.

"Beautiful Venice, Bride of the Sea!"

A girl, who must have learned the old, old ballad from her grandmother's music-books, was singing it in a flexible mezzo-soprano on the Lagoon last night, under the full moon. Other voices made the chorus a part-song. The mellow harmonies are with us still:

"Beautiful Venice! City of Song!
What wonders of old to thy regions belong!
What sweet recollections cling to my heart
As thy fast-fading shores from my vision depart.
Oh, Poesy's home is thy light colonnade
  Where the winds gently sigh and the sweet twilights fade.
I have known many homes, but the dwelling for me
  Is Beautiful Venice, the Bride of the Sea!"

The ripple and languorous swing of the melody must have been thought out by the composer on such a night, and under such a moon, and upon such waters as recalled it to the girl with the sympathetic mezzo-soprano voice. All unwittingly she

made us her grateful debtors.   The words
are not poetry ; the air is not music.   Yet
we account it of more value than a hundred
modern *canzonettas* and barcaroles.

The retrospective murmur of the re-
frain is the prelude to our Story.

It begins in the bewitching old way—
Once upon a Time.   The Once and the
Time are as worn and discoloured by the
wash of centuries as the rocks of the ruined quay, but as firm as the piles driven
into the heart of the earth and upbearing
the Campanile, Duomo and Baptistery of
the waste Island City.

In that Once of the thousand-year-old
Time, Orseoli, Doge of Venice, wrought
for her fame and power exceeding all that
his predecessors had gained.   Under his
leadership the Bride of the Adriatic became the Queen of every sea ploughed by
her victorious galleys, and their range
comprised all of the known world.   Kings
came bending unto her, and those who
had despised her youth and poverty,
bowed at her white feet, and all men
spoke well of her greatest Captain and

wisest ruler.   Heaven had set the seal of
Divine favor upon his works and ways by
giving him a large family of noble sons
and virtuous daughters.   The heir apparent, Giovanni, a brave and accomplished
youth, was invited to Constantinople by
the Emperors, Basil and Constantine, and
was there married to one of the Royal
house.   After he brought her to Venice
"with great pomp and festivity," he was
associated with his father in the government of the State, an appointment that
made yet more stable the throne established upon the seas, and apparently as
stable as the girdle of snow-topped Alps
bounding the north-western horizon of the
Great Republic.

Next to Giovanni among the Doge's
sons, stood Orso, the scholar *par eminence*
in a household where all were emulous in
learning, and patrons of the fine arts.   His
choice of the priesthood as a sphere for his
talents and ambitions, was not opposed by
the father.   He had, besides Giovanni, another son, Otto, to make the succession
sure, even after the youngest, Vitale, had

also gone into holy orders, and a daughter, for whom the Emperor Otto II. had stood godfather in San Marco, determined to take the veil. The Church was the twin of the State in dignity and authority. When Orso was made Bishop of the island-parish of Torcello—the Torcello acknowledged and revered as the Mother of Venice—the Doge smiled, well-pleased, upon the zeal with which the new incumbent set about rebuilding her Cathedral in a style so far surpassing its earlier estate that nothing in Venice approached it in design and execution. Had the veined marble pillars, combining with Corinthian capitals reminiscences of the Byzantium that was ever the loving ally of the Orseoli ; the exquisitely wrought rood-screen, copied, in part, by the architects of San Marco, dividing the choir from the body of the church, and the Episcopal throne, or Bishop's Seat, commanding the whole interior, been the work of Orso's own hands, he could have left us no more definite expression of his mind, character, and tastes. All is noble, pure, and elevated. In the

minutest detail we discern the singleness
of devotion to his high calling and to his
diocese which changed desolation into a
miracle of beauty.

About the Cathedral group sprang up
and flourished a miniature realm informed
by his energy and refinement.

" Behind the high altar, on the Bishop's
high cold throne overlooking the great temple, he sat among his presbyters and con-
trolled the counsels and led the decisions
of a community then active and wealthy,"
says a careful chronicler.

While Torcello, thus transformed, was
to him wife, child, and kingdom, his inter-
course with father and brothers was always
close and tender. The old Doge took
counsel with this, his gravest and most judicious son, in affairs of state. When the
plague fell, like a black frost from heaven,
upon prosperous Venice, blighting, among
the first victims, Giovanni, his wife and
their baby-boy, Orso's strong heart was his
father's stay ; his clear brain was ready
with a measure that should effectually
avert the calamity of panic and anarchy.

13

Otto, the Doge's third son, was the *protégé* of Otto II., whose visit, *incognito*, to Pietro Orseoli, the great Doge, is one of the romantic incidents of Venetian history.   As a boy, he had been solemnly sent to Verona for confirmation, the Emperor, on that occasion, exchanging the child's name of " Pietro " for the Emperor's own, "in sign of high favour and affection."   After this, the lad spent much of his time at Court, and before he was twenty, married a Hungarian princess.   The annalists of this period exhaust their store of adjectival epithets in praise of his gifts of person, intellect, and heart.   He was " Catholic in faith, strong in justice, eminent in religion, decorous in his way of living, great in riches, and so full of all kinds of goodness that, by his merits, he was judged of all to be the most fit successor of his excellent father and blesséd grandfather,"—is the tribute of one historian.

Otto was but a lad—hardly eighteen, according to some authorities—when Giovanni, his princess-bride, and their infant heir, were swept away at one breath of

BISHOP'S THRONE IN CATHEDRAL OF TORCELLO. BUILT BY ORSO ORSEOLI.

the destroyer.   Orso, whose especial pupil
and darling the younger brother was, was
audacious in recommending that he should
share their father's authority, but he knew
Otto, and, it may be, was as well advised
as to his own personal influence in Venice.
Nevertheless, it was a perilous eminence
on which the young fellow was left alone
by his father's death.   This occurred
within a couple of years after that of
Giovanni, and the Venetians, kept quiet
by the munificent bequest of the late Doge
of one half of his fortune, " for the use
and solace of all the poor in the Republic,"
yielded what looked like willing obedience
to his successor for fifteen years.   In all
this time, his intimacy with, and depend-
ence upon, Orso, were so evident that
they seemed to rule as one man.   Orso
was now Patriarch of Grado, the highest
preferment in the gift of the Church.   The
Orseoli virtually owned the Republic, and
there were hundreds of men as ambitious,
if less worthy, who envied them with all
the rancor of disappointed politicians and
ecclesiastical aspirants.

The terrible truth that trouble came first to Otto through an attack upon himself, seems never to have been absent from Orso's memory from the beginning of their reverses. The Doge had ruled with exemplary moderation; had been sagacious in counsel and intrepid in military and naval movements, and remained singularly unspoiled by the honors crowded and packed upon him from his childhood up. The machinery of government, ordained and regulated by his father, had worked so well and so long that we are startled by the jar that threw it out of balance. A rival and belligerent Patriarch, Poppo of Aquileia, after cunningly undermining the influence of both brothers among the easily-stirred populace, boldly accused Orso to the Pope as one who had been illegally appointed to his high office, and was a wilful accessory in the unlawful act. The Venetians had taken too much for granted in their attachment to the intriguing and powerful Orseoli. The good of the Church and the integrity of the State, so long dom-

inated by the lordly race, demanded investigation into, and summary righting of,
this and divers other wrongs.

A popular tumult was incited by the
crafty insinuations. To accuse Orso was
to involve Otto, and he would not be
likely to listen calmly to aspersions of his
best-beloved brother. " Great discord between the Venetians and the Doge," was
the inevitable consequence of the attempted investigation. In breathless succession ensued Orso's resignation of the
Patriarchate, and Otto's abdication of the
office of Doge. Indignant at the ingrati-
tude of those who owed their house so
much, they did not wait to be tried or de-
posed. Withdrawing voluntarily from the
scene of violent disquiet, they retired to
Istria, and left Venice to her fate.

The panic and anarchy warded off by
Otto's appointment to the place vacated
by Giovanni's death, swooped down upon
the ungoverned city, breeding such extremity of misery that a piteous recall was
sent to the self-expatriated pair within a
twelvemonth after their departure. Poppo

had gained possession of Grado by promises of peaceful protection of the citizens, and, once in, sacked and insulted her
as a conqueror.   Otto was recalled in hot,
repentant haste, put the invaders to flight,
and re-entered Venice in calm triumph.

The work of restoration was not thor-
ough for some reason that is lost to us in
the mingling dust of the ages.   Orso's
rehabilitation was cleaner and closer building than Otto's resumption of sovereignty.
His stirred nest was unskilfully relaid.
He may have been deficient in the discre-
tion that waits upon advance in years, or
the lesson of magnanimity he might have
learned from his elder brother, may have
been imperfectly conned.   The fever of
popular reactionary enthusiasm, remitted
when the system was reduced by blood-
letting and famine, arose again before
Otto was fairly re-established in his father's
seat.   His second exile was flight, and a
necessity.   Orso was again his companion,
and, as before, of his own free will.   Having remained with his brother until he
was safe, and hospitably lodged in Con-

stantinople, the brave priest returned to
Venice, and gave himself resolutely to the
work of clearing Otto's dear name from
obloquy, and bringing back the distracted
dupes of designing traitors to allegiance
to their rightful ruler.

Through one revolution, and yet another,
and another, he never relaxed his intention.   It may well be conceived how loath-
some to a man of clean life and scholarly
tastes, must have been the contact with
the elements that fought against him.
Standing deep in the muck of Venetian
politics, his soul must have yearned un-
speakably for peace and Torcello ; for the
pastoral simplicity of the life he had put
behind him, the trustful affection of the
flock he had led and fed like a shep-
herd.

Whether or not his sacrifices and their
end were comprehended by the Venetians,
and his lofty patriotism moved them to
shame, we cannot say.   Their first token
of a saner mood was in the earnest, even
abject, petition to him to accept the
Doge's place and name, and to hold it in

trust until an embassy could be sent to bring Otto home.

Venice never did a wiser thing than in inducting the Patriarch Orso into the office his grandfather, father, and brother had filled in the best days of the mighty Republic. Trained to statecraft in these successive administrations, early admitted to the honour of consultation with Pietro Orseoli, and acting, for years, as Otto's unofficial counsellor, while he combined in himself the finest qualities of his predecessors—he was able to lay upon the helm a hand that brought the ship of State out of the tempest and into such calm waters as she had not known through many a dark and cloudy day. Born to the purple, he proved to be a leader born, and not made by the exigencies of the national crisis.

To Vitale, the youngest of the four brothers, was committed the grateful task of heading the embassy to Constantinople and of conducting the exile in honour to home and people. It was a long voyage, and the trusty galleys, at their best, lagged

far behind the eager flight of Orso's de-
sires to see the culmination of his holy
emprise.   I think no man, since the corner-
stone of human history was laid, ever
knew purer exultation of hope than must
have sprung eternal in his brother-heart
through that year of waiting and working
and watching.

Presently—for we are nearing the island
—we will climb to the top of the rude
Campanile he had left as it was when he
rebuilt the Duomo, and look—as tradition
says and, we doubt not, truly, he was
wont to gaze, whenever he could escape
from Venice and State cares—over "the
paleness and the roar of the Adriatic,"
sweeping the shifting distances with eyes
full of fond anticipation, and faint with
longing.   How often he dreamed over
the meeting that would follow upon the
first glimpse of the masts and sails of the
homeward-bound fleet, we shall not trust
ourselves to think in the knowledge of
what the end of labour and dreaming was
to be.

As happily and as hopefully he beheld

the increasing wealth and tranquillity of the
realm he would resign into Otto's hands
in the fulness of God's time. Every
evil overcome, every success achieved,
was one more love-gift for the boy, dearer
than life and fame, and than Torcello
itself, to the man who would never hold
son of his own in his arms.

The fleet came home.

Let us tell the rest briefly.

Otto was dead in exile. He had never
known that Orso was making and keeping his rightful place for him, much less
how well the work was done, or in what
sublimity of love and faith he had awaited
the hour when his best-beloved should
have his own again.

The sharp prow of our gondola pushes
aside the branches of flowering "May,"
—the sweet English hawthorn, lining the
inlet we have entered—and cuts into the
sedges drooping and dripping in the dead
water about the landing-place. The island
is as flat as a table-top, and little above
the wash of the tide. The cluster of
church-buildings stands in a grassy square.

The surrounding meadows are whitened by the Bethlehem stars. A few mean cottages dot them, the homes of the hundred-and-fifty farm-labourers who till the fields they do not own. The Mother of Venice sits, a Madonna Dolorosa to the pitying few who come to muse upon what she was to him who loved her best, and who took refuge here when his beautiful hope died a violent death.

From the Campanile we turn our thoughtful steps to his tomb in front of the high altar. Upon it is his effigy, in strong basso-relievo. The Patriarch's mitre is upon his head.

Did the peace stamped upon the face, worn with thought and time, settle there with the death-shadow? or did the gentle monotony of his priestly functions, the society of his brother in faith and in blood, who succeeded him in the Bishopric of Torcello, and his sister the Lady Abbess, " with perhaps a humbler nun or two of the same blood "—like the stroke of mesmeric finger-tips over tortured nerves, finally assuage the sharpness of his pain, and soften the memory of the murder of the beautiful hope? And so did Torcello begin to be for his comfort?

There is no inscription upon the memorial-slab. We could not bring ourselves to read it if there were. That his end was peace, and that his memory was blesséd with those who laid him here, full of years and honours, we already know. Before we set foot in his island bishopric, we had settled within ourselves what words would have been graven here, had the beautiful hope lived and not perished, and Otto the Doge closed the Patriarch Orso's eyes for his last sleep:

"*Thy love to me was wonderful, passing the love of women.*"

XII

IN RAVENNA

XII

IN RAVENNA

WE run down from Bologna to Ravenna by rail. The track is laid along the line of a Roman road constructed before the Christian era. The landscape is placid in beauty, although monotonous. The May haying is in progress ; mowers stand waist-deep in millet and barley and in clover that is tipped with purple spikes instead of bobbing pink heads ; the barefooted women raking the swaths into heaps are picturesque in red jackets and orange-coloured petticoats. Each field is separated from the rest by what we name " one-legged dancers,"—pollarded mulberry- and fig-trees, joined by festoons of vines, vibrating in the gentle breeze that shows the lining of flaming poppies under the ruffled skirts of the standing grain. A scarlet binding of the same follows the road-bed, and the wide picture of peace and plenteousness has a frame of mountains, benignant in outline, rich in tint and shading.

At long intervals the white walls of a villa and a cluster of grey farm-buildings break up the green uniformity of the distances, near and remote ; or the train halts at a château of the fifteenth century, now a railway station, or a town that was the birthplace of an archbishop who died about 490 A.D. and of a painter who saw the light two years after Columbus discovered America, and cannot, therefore, be numbered with the ancients.

The sun-filled air is as delicious to the lungs as the harmonious wealth of colour to the sight. Verdure and mountain-range, sunlight, and the atmosphere cooled by wandering breaths from the sea we are nearing, and from snow-caps, of which we get furtive glimpses between lower peaks, —were the same when Dante trod his lonely way from Bologna in 1319, and when Byron travelled by post-chaise over this very route in the month of June, 1819.

The house in which he took up his abode upon his arrival in Ravenna is one of the show-places of the town. Our cabman drives us from the station, first, to the Martyr's Monument, erected in 1888 to the memory of Garibaldi's wife Anita, who died in 1849, with her unborn child, of hardships and exposure while hiding in the Ravenna marshes from those who sought her husband's life. Next, we are taken to the Cathedral, rebuilt in the eighteenth century upon the foundations of a church older than itself by twelve hundred years. Thirdly, we go to the Casa di Lord Byron.

It is now a café, bearing (of course) his name, and, to suit the requirements of the present occupants, the interior has been materially altered. Externally, it remains as it was seventy-odd years ago. It is two-storied, of fair dimensions, and perfectly plain in architecture; the stone walls are coated with the buff stucco which is the livery of two-thirds of the private houses and most of the hotels in Italy. The arched doorway is the same from which

14

the handsome English aristocrat emerged
daily for his lounge through the quaint,
shadowy streets, or his gallop in the
Pineta, and sallied forth duly after supper
for the evening call upon the Countess
Guiccioli, never omitted in the stormiest
weather. The common people of Ravenna
used to nudge one another as Dante
passed, and whisper to their children that
the stranger with the swarthy skin and
rapt eyes came and went to hell whenever he pleased to make the journey.
The haughty beauty and exclusive habits
of the foreign lord who had chosen, for no
reason that they could divine, a residence
in their out-of-the-way city, must have
moved the bourgeois gossips to conjectures
as absurd, until the secret of the magnet
that kept him here became public property.

"Lord Byron preferred Ravenna to all
the other towns of Italy, and was influenced
in some measure by his intimacy with the
Countess Guiccioli, a member of the
Gamba family of Ravenna," says Bae-
deker, primly, and lets the story pass.

The said "member" of a noble house

BYRON'S HOUSE IN RAVENNA.

did not acquiesce in the disposition of charitable *ciceroni* to smooth out one of the ugliest creases in a life that was badly "laundered" throughout. On the contrary, she calls attention peremptorily to the length and breadth and depth of the social blemish by means of two ponderous volumes, penned ostensibly—and ostentatiously—by her own hand in wordy Italian, and done into English by an abnormally patient translator. The work is incorrigibly stupid, and inconceivably moralistic, when one considers who was the author and who the subject of the memoir. Skipping as lightly as the heaviness of the soil will allow, over the chapters devoted to Lord Byron's constancy, his lofty sense of honour, his religious convictions, his marital magnanimity, and his filial piety, we extract from the account of his life in Ravenna certain details which further the purpose we had in visiting the sad and hoary town.

The book is opened upon our luncheon-table in the dining-room of the Hotel Lord Byron, hard by Casa and café. It

is a cheerful, commodious little caravan-
sery, flanked by a garden gay with roses,
jasmine, honeysuckle, and azaleas.   Out of
a gorgeous tangle of these rises a fine
marble bust of Byron, taken—as we
would fain depict him to ourselves, even
here, if we could—at his best.

"The Countess G——," as she delicately designates herself, writes modestly
in the third person and makes it plain,
unintentionally and unconsciously, that
other attractions besides hers had part in
bringing Byron to Ravenna, if not in
detaining him here.

He had been an inmate of No. 225
Strada di Porta Sisi for some weeks before he became intimate with the inmates
of the Palazzo Guiccioli, Via di Porta
Adriana.   What followed we give in the
titled author's own words:

"He was requested by Count G——
to accompany his young wife into society,
to the play, everywhere in short.   Soon
Lord Byron took up his abode in their
palace, and the repose of heart and mind
he thus attained was so great that no sad-

ness seemed able to come near him so long as this tranquil, regular, pleasing sort of existence lasted."

The chapter embodying this choice excerpt bears the caption, *The Melancholy of Lord Byron*. The naïve presumption upon her readers' sympathy in the lament over the untoward circumstances that induced his relapse into the slough of despond must provoke a smile from the most puritanical of us all. We are left to glean from other sources the trivial facts of the trusting husband's awakening to the relations existing between the wife who was many years his junior, and his honoured guest and friend, promoted by the unsuspecting old noble to the position of her *cavaliere servente*.

Byron's residence in the Palazzo Guiccioli came to an unpleasant end, and he returned to his old quarters.

"The Countess G—— obtained from his Holiness Pius VII., at the petition of her parents, permission to leave her husband and return home to her family," is our next item of disconnected information, and that, while his fair friend lived quietly in a country house, Byron " was now reduced to solitude in the same place her presence had gladdened."

"Ravenna," continues the Countess G——, "which is always a sad kind of abode, becomes in autumn quite a desert, liable to fever. There was no longer a single being with whom he could exchange a word or a thought."

Equinoctial storms of wind and rain prevented him from seeking solace in his favourite diversions of boating, swimming, and riding. The Casa Lord Byron, sodden with rain outside until the buff walls were a jaundiced yellow, while the sea-winds, driving in at the casement seams and under the doors over the stone floors, made the interior as bleak as the drenched outer world, must have been a sorry place, difficult to conceive of amid the bloom and brightness of the Italian garden before our eyes.

"This season kills me with sadness," the *ennuyéed* exile wrote to the Countess G——, September 20, 1820. "When I have my mental malady it is well for others to keep away. Love me! My soul is like the leaves that fall in autumn—all yellow."

He had more active causes for discontent as the weeks went on. Dreading few things more than a return to the England he had sworn he would never see again, he regarded with repugnance the probability that he might be summoned as a witness in the trial of Queen Caroline, then pending in the English courts. His letters kept him uneasy on this head, and furthermore contained news of the dangerous illness of his illegitimate daughter Allegra, who, happily for her, died some months later. Side by side with these troubles, the Countess G—— sets the grave fact that, notwithstanding the gracious decree of Pius VII., she "continued to be tormented by her husband, who refused to accept the decision of Rome because he did not wish for a separation." Also, that "the Papal Government, pushed on by the Austrian police, had recourse to a thousand small, vexatious measures to make Lord Byron quit Ravenna, where he had given offence by becoming too popular with the Liberal Party."

The weather of that winter is described as " extraordinary. Snow and sirocco one day ; ice and snow the other." On account of a misunderstanding with his English publisher and agent, Byron's letters and papers were not forwarded to Ravenna for several weeks together.

" His sole amusement consisted in stirring the fire and playing with Lion, his mastiff, or with his little menagerie."

Don Juan had been published anonymously, and a new anxiety beset him on hearing that Shelley had been adjudged unfit to have the guardianship of his child in consequence of his atheistic writings. Ada Byron, by the terms of her parents' separation, was to be allowed to communicate with and to see her father at his will, when she should reach the age of eighteen. Byron wrote urgently to his publishers not to allow the authorship of his poem to transpire.

"I prefer my child to a poem at any time."

A prey to " the worm, the canker, and
the grief," he lived out the lowering days,
with no prospect from his windows save
the dripping blank walls of the opposite
houses, chilled to the bone and to the
heart. Yet a half-smile of contempt curls
our lips in reading that his evening visit
to the Countess G——, who had again
taken up her abode in Ravenna, was the
only light that crossed his shadowed path.
One passage is almost pastoral in guileless
phraseology :

" A few simple airs played by her on the
piano, some slight diversion, such as a ray
of sunshine between two showers, or a star
in the heavens, raising hopes of a brighter
morrow, sufficed to clear up his horizon."

The effect of the sketch, dashed in with
these few touches of the artistic brush,
would be pleasing were it not for sundry
inconvenient memories which break up
unities and injure perspectives.

In 1816 Byron had studied the Armen-
ian language because he " found that his
mind wanted something craggy to break
upon," and he had chosen this rugged

tongue "to torture him into attention."
To the same end, he began, and finished,
Sardanapalus in Ravenna.

The Countess G—— had gone to Florence and Pisa upon a visit of some length,
and her letters, " pregnant with alarm and
affliction lest Lord Byron should be assas-
sinated at Ravenna," did not abate the
melancholy that settled upon his spirit like
the miasmatic mists of the marshes across
which he galloped every passably fine day
to the "long alleys of imperial pines."

In the absence of his fair friend, the
most brilliant and the most miserable man
of his day had his evenings again upon his
hands, and with no companions except
faithful Lion and the trooping memories
at which we have hinted.　They had been
busy and relentless on the night preceding
the anniversary of a day he had cursed
many a time, and more savagely than in
the mood that prompted lines whose power
and pathos lie in their sincerity and lack
of art :

"To-morrow is my birthday.　That is
to say, at twelve of the clock, midnight—

i. e., in twelve minutes, I shall have completed thirty-three years of age !!! and I
go to my bed with a heaviness of heart at
having lived so long, and to so little purpose. . . . I do not regret this year for
what I have done, but for what I have *not*
done."

The tablet above the door of the Casa
Lord Byron was inserted in the wall many
years after the death of him who made
the homely building classic. We copy part
of it from our seat in the carriage we have
engaged to take us to the Pineta after we
have visited the Tomb of Dante on the
next corner :

LORD BYRON,

Splendore del Secolo Decimonono
E di nostre glorie poeta nell' insuperato Child
　　Harold
Questa Casa il 10 Giugno 1819 a sua duiora eletta
Perche vicina alla Tomba di Dante Alighieri
Otto mesi abitava mal sapendosi dividere
Dall' immortale dell' Italia indipendenza initiatore
E dall' famosa ed unica Pinetà.

(LORD BYRON,

Splendour of the nineteenth century, and

poet of our glories in the unsurpassed Childe Harold, selected this house as his dwelling, June 10, 1819, because near to the tomb of Dante Alighieri.   He lived in it eight months, hardly knowing how to part from the immortal initiator of Italian independence and from the famous and unique Pineta.)

Byron tells us :

"I pass each day where Dante's bones are laid ;
A little cupola, more neat than solemn,
Protects his dust."

Within the last forty years we have learned that the "neat" tomb before which the brother-bard must have mused a thousand times, and upon which he laid a sheaf of his own poems in reverent sympathy with the transports that drove Alfieri to his knees at the base of the monument crowned by the august profile in *basso rilievo*, — did not then hold Dante's bones, or so much as a handful of his ashes.

"The story of his burial, and of the discovery of his real tomb is fresh in the

DANTÈ'S TOMB IN RAVENNA.

memory of everyone," writes John Addington Symonds, in his exquisite monograph upon Ravenna.

We have heard several versions of the tale, but these were so contradictory and garbled that we gratefully avail ourselves of more direct information, in the shape of a history of Ravenna bought here and recommended as trustworthy by competent judges of historic records. The account herein given is, perhaps, far more interesting to us than to Mr. Symonds's better-read audience. Especially when the rough translation I take the liberty to append herewith is rendered low and rapidly within the very precincts of the small temple, our skirts brushing the shrine and, through the open door, the sunshine falling aslant upon the familiar lineaments of the Mighty Master:

"From the end of the fourteenth century until 1865, incessant demands were made by Florence for the bones of the Poet, that they might be reverently deposited in the Church of Santa Croce. But the love and just pride which moved that city to demand this, determined Ravenna to refuse it. When, however, Ravenna was once more under the power of the Popes, and a Medici, under the name of Leo X., mounted the papal throne, the danger that the precious skeleton might be rifled from its niche became imminent. In fact, Leo X., in 1519, granted permission to the Florentines to open the sepulchre of Dante, take up the remains, and transport them to their own country. When the commissioners arrived, and the urn was opened, they found only a few leaves of laurel and aloes and a little dust.

"They beheld, also, that in the side of the arch backed by the wall of the convent [Franciscan] there was a fissure, and comprehended that the Franciscans had foiled them by working from the inside of the cloister and removing the bones. The regrets of the Florentines were great, and continued under the reign of Clement VII. [another Medici], but he was engrossed by too many and too serious political complications to occupy himself with the bones of a poet. These re-

mained within the monastery, in the
jealous custody of the brethren, who
transmitted them from one generation to
the other, making at intervals a recognition
[*recognizione*]. One of these was made
by Father Antonio Santi, in 1677, and
another, it appears, in 1723, by Father
Guardiano Pallavese. Those who believed that Father Santi concealed the
casket he had made containing the bones,
within the walled gate where they were
found in 1865, were mistaken. This gate
was opened in 1701, hardly a quarter-
century after the *recognizione* of Father
Santi, and remained open to give access
to the old cemetery during the entire century. Everything indicates that the bones
were hidden where they afterward came
to light as late as 1810. That is, when
the Franciscans, under the new law of
suppression, departed with no hope of
return. It is certainly known that one
Father Amadori went about shortly after,
saying 'there was to be found in Braccio-
forte *a great treasure.*' . . .

"In 1865, the year in which occurred

the sixth centenary of Dante's birth, the
Commune set about the demolition of a
small church near the tomb of the Poet.
In this work they found that part of the
wall corresponded with the wall of the
Franciscan monastery. Five urns were
discovered here, the statue of Guardarello
Guardarelli, and, in a walled-up gate, a
portion of which is now preserved in an
enclosure of Istria stone, the coffer containing the bones of Dante. . . . This
wooden casket in which, in 1677, Father
Antonio Santi deposited the bones of
Dante . . . after the *recognizione*, is
still preserved in the library."

We are led out of the temple tomb
into an adjoining area, where the custodian unlocks a door in the side of the
oblong "enclosure of Istria stone," that
we may see the former hiding-place of
the hoarded and hunted mortal part of
Dante,—a wanderer and fugitive in death
as in life.

It is all infinitely pitiable, but our regrets are not with "ungrateful Florence"
in "the remorse of ages" that found ex-

pression in the unseemly game of hide-
and-seek.

From Byron's house and Dante's tomb,
we turn our faces, naturally, to the Pineta
of To-day, the Pinetum of a Past so old
we are dizzied in the thinking of it.

Ravenna was a Roman naval station
before Christ, and before that was a pro-
totype of Venice in situation, wealth, and
beauty, "standing in the centre of a huge
lagoon, the fresh waters of the Ronco
and the Po mixing with the salt waves of
the Adriatic around its very walls." The
sea has receded sullenly as riches and
population have deserted the doomed
city, until she lies stranded six miles, as
the crow flies, from the nearest beach.
Shrunken and decrepit, her only pulse of
commerce is a sluggish canal, ten miles
long, down which a few small vessels
creep to the Adriatic.

Wood for the galleys of Augustus, for
those of the consuls who went before, and
for the ships of those who wore the imperial purple after him, was cut in the
Pinetum, then forty miles in length, and

15

five or six in width.   We are told,—and
we credit it, at sight of the remaining
monarchs, lifting their palmy brows to
heaven,—that these pines did not gain
maturity in height, in heart, and in girth
under three centuries of growth.   After a
five miles' drive over a depressing level,
we catch sight of this remnant of departed
grandeur.   To our apprehension it vies in
mournful magnificence with the unfading
mosaics of agèd Ravenna.

Half-way between the town and the
old boundary of the Pinetum is a church
founded in memory of an immediate successor of the Apostles, who suffered martyrdom here " *July 23, 79 !* "   The flat,
long road is a mere causeway, bordered,
for a couple of miles, by fertile fields and
farm-cottages, after that by festering fens
that breed deadly fevers in summer and
autumn.   Like the fickle sea, the pine
forest has retreated from the city of which
it was formerly the inimitable ornament.
We gain the impression, in looking back
to her and forward to the solemn border
of blackish-green cutting into the sky-line,

that the two were in an unholy compact
in leaving the discrowned queen to die
slowly and alone.

Our cab-driver calls the weary route
five miles long. We know it to be ten
before we alight at the outermost rank
of the ancient giants. The terrible frosts
in the winter of 1880–81 killed great trees
by the hundred, and younger by the
thousand. In 1895, a fire, kindled by
some wood-cutters, got away from them
and burned up so much of what the frost
had left that a scanty fringe, between
seven and eight miles in length and less
than a mile broad, is all we have left of
"what existed in the time of Odoacer
and has been extolled by Dante, Boccaccio, Dryden, and Byron."

Sweet-hearted Nature, nowhere more
generous than in Italy, is doing her best,
and in loving haste, to rebuild the waste
places. Thickets of hawthorn and wild
roses have grown up again among the
columnar boles of the larger trees ; creep-
ing vines, some of which we know by
sight and name, although most of them

are as strange as they are lovely, run
lithely up to the lower boughs and fling
out flowering pendants in the balm-laden
air.   The breath of the balsamic trees is
a catholicon in the very heart of the pesti-
lential district.   Miasmatic currents from
the marshes never pass the charmed ram-
parts.   We pick up brown cones with
closely knit scales, glossy, as from varnish,
and of surprising weight.   They are laden,
we are informed, with the chief wealth of
the neighbouring peasantry, the toothsome
kernels of the stone-pine, popular with
Italian cooks, and with confectioners everywhere.   The ground is carpeted by mosses
and wild-flowers; now and then a bird
sends a melodious trill or cadenza from
arbors no man has planted or woven.
Among the evergreen rafters and groin-
ings of the roof, a hundred feet above
our heads, the music goes on forever,—
anthem, chant, *Miserere*, and *Te Deum*,—
a magnificent surge of sound, movements,
and numbers that were old when the world
was young.

"Harpers, harping with their harps,"

quotes one, softly.

Another,—

"The Wind—that grand old harper—smote
His thunder-harp of pines."

For us, Dante walks still beneath the boughs that combine into our cathedral-roof. "*Che inspirò già il Divino,*" is a clause in the tablet upon Byron's house in Ravenna. The English poet's love for the

"————solitude
Of the pine-forest, and the silent shore
Which bounds Ravenna's immemorial wood,
Rooted where once the Adrian wave flowed o'er
To where the last Cæsarean fortress stood,"

puts words into our mouths and gentler charity into our hearts as we, too, stroll and dream.

XIII

IL MAGNIFICO

XIII

IL MAGNIFICO

IT was a Pazzo who brought to Florence a torch kindled at the fire that comes down yearly from Heaven to the Holy Sepulchre in Jerusalem. With fine disregard of distances by sea and land, and the non-existence of swift transit facilities a thousand-and-odd years ago, the legend relates how the then obscure adventurer transported the sacred fire at full gallop all the way from the church built by Constantine at the behest of his mother, Helena, to Santa Reparata, on the site of which the Duomo of Florence now stands.

When within a few miles of the city he perceived that the current of air created by his breakneck zeal endangered the life of the blazing flambeau. Whereupon,

without checking his speed, he wheeled
about in the saddle and dashed into the
city, facing the horse's tail, thus screening
the flickering fire with his body.

"See the *pazzo* (crazy fellow) !" hooted
the mob.

From which outcry, when the truth was
known,—and the pious ingenuity of the
rider was rewarded by the thanks of the
Church and the freedom of the city, with
a palace and a fortune thrown in to weight
the empty honours,—the house that became a power in the State took the name
of Pazzi, and bore it boastfully forever
afterward.

This is the story revived in Florence
upon each Easter-even, when all the world
crowds to the Cathedral to witness the
spectacle some dead-and-gone-ages-ago
Pazzi—perhaps the original torchbearer
—left money to perpetuate to the end of
time, or as long as people are willing to
be fooled, which amounts to the same
thing.

We saw it, a month ago, in the Duomo
where Savonarola used to preach against

priestly follies and vain amusements, and lies of all sorts. A tall pole was held upright in the central aisle by wires; other wires ran from it to the high altar and to the great front door, the whole length of the building. The crowd, like all holiday Italian crowds, was good-humoured, courteous, and patient of the hour's delay between the time set for the exhibition and its actual occurrence. Mass was going on before the altar. Gleams of moving candles, the white sacques of choir-boys, and the tinselled copes and stoles of the officiating priests were visible in the gaps of the throng. A few of those who were near enough to see what was passing there, knelt and bowed, from time to time, rather politely than devoutly. Snatches of responsive chanting arose above, and punctuated, the hum of talk and the indescribable rustle of moving human bodies as the press became solid from wall to wall. The palpitating mass parted, and without disorder, to clear the aisle for a procession of priests and acolytes with tapers and one odd-looking pennon fast-

ened to a long staff, marching slowly,
chanting as they passed, to the door and
so out into the square. Their errand was
to bless the pyramidal car, wreathed with
flowers and strung with fireworks, awaiting the coming of the sacred flame from
the altar. The four immense cream-col-
oured oxen with garlanded horns, attached
to the car, shared in the benediction.

The procession marched back to the
chancel, and, within a decent interval after
this return, a glare of electric light lit up
the building; a rocket whizzed shrilly
along the central wire, showering sparks
as it flew, and through the entrance to the
peak of the car. Then, amid the banging
and popping and hissing that filled the
great dome with smoke and reverbera-
tion, it sped back to the tall pole, its mis-
sion accomplished. The rocket is known
as the " Dove." The exhibition would
be puerile and undignified at a Fourth of
July celebration in a mining-camp of the
rudest West. It signifies the descent of
the holy fire which we, of this practical
century, are asked to believe is miracu-

lously kindled annually in the (alleged) Holy Sepulchre.

Dove, pyrotechnics, and legend are sanctioned by the Mother Church, and the "show" is ushered in by religious services in a consecrated temple. The *sequitur* is the slow, lumbering progress of the car drawn by the blessèd oxen, to the Pazzi palace, in grateful recognition of the munificence that bestowed one more *festa* upon the Italian populace.

The Pazzi, at a much later date in Florentine history, played a leading part in another and far dissimilar scene in this same Duomo. The names of Francesco and Jacopo Pazzi were prominent among the ringleaders of the conspiracy against the lives of Lorenzo de' Medici (Il Magnifico) and his favourite brother, Giuliano— "a kindly youth whose only fault was that he belonged to the cursèd line of the Medici." The nephews of the reigning Pontiff, Sixtus V., the Archbishop of Pisa, and divers of the lesser clergy, were mixed up with the plot to assassinate the brothers upon Sunday, April 26, 1478. The moment fixed upon (let us hope not by papal authority) was that when, in the course of the evening service, the Host should be elevated by the priest above the kneeling congregation.   Lorenzo was "told off" to the dagger of a reverend accomplice, while the Pazzi undertook to despatch Giuliano.

We have read the tragedy in a dozen different books, and always with a throb of keenest pity for the inoffensive youth, who fell a swift and bloody sacrifice to his detested name.   In my girlhood I hung spellbound over a historical novelette that had its *denouement* in the Cathedral murder. I have forgotten author and title.   I shall never forget the story of Francesco Pazzi's call for Giuliano at the house of the latter, that the conspirators might be sure of his attendance at the evening service, and the incident of the false friend's impulsive embrace of his smiling dupe, that he might know whether or not he wore a shirt of mail under his silken doublet.

The very words of the novelist have stayed by me all these years.

" Reassured by the warmth and softness of the unprotected flesh, he let his hand slip from Giuliano's shoulder to his arm, and the two walked on gayly, side-by-side, to the Cathedral, already thronged with worshippers."

The younger of the Medicean brothers was stabbed to the heart by Francesco de' Pazzi at the given signal. In kneeling at the lifting of the Host, Giuliano bowed himself in death. The assassin struck again to make sure of his deadly purpose, and in his awkward violence lamed himself by a cut in the thigh. The priest's attack upon Lorenzo was yet more clumsy, inflicting only a flesh-wound in the neck. Although taken at such cruel disadvantage, Lorenzo defended himself so well that he and the two friends who had accompanied him to the Cathedral—Politian, the poet and scholar, and Antonio Ridolfi, a Florentine noble—fought their way to the sacristy and barred the door against their assailants. Once secure in their asylum, Ridolfi's first action was to apply his lips to the cut in his patron's neck, to draw out the venom should the priestly poniard have been poisoned.

Foiled of their prey, the assassins rushed into the streets of the town, calling upon the oppressed people to rise against the Medicean tyrant, Jacopo de' Pazzi shouting, "Freedom! and down with the *palle!* (the balls that were the armourial bearings of the Medici)." The effort to rally those whose coöperation they had a right to expect was, like the demonstration in the Duomo, a pitiable failure.

In the highly dramatic sketch of the unsuccessful plot given in Howells's *Tuscan Cities,*—than which no other volume of travel conveys to us more faithfully the very breath and colour of Florentine life,— the bungler, Francesco, is apostrophised with graphic bitterness :

" Pick yourself up, Francesco Pazzi, and get home as you may ! There is no mounting to horse and crying liberty through the streets for you ! All is over ! The wretched populace, the servile signory, side with the Medici. In a few

hours the Archbishop of Pisa is swinging
by the neck from a window of the Palazzo
Vecchio ; and while he is yet alive, you
are dragged, bleeding and naked, from
your bed through the streets and hung
beside him, so close that, in his dying
agony, he sets his teeth in your breast
with a convulsive frenzy that leaves you
fast in the death-clutch of his jaws till
they cut the ropes, and you run hideously
down to the pavement below."

One has need to draw a deep, painful
breath between this passage and the next
chapter, a necessity acknowledged by the
author in the introductory sentence :

" One must face these grisly details
from time to time, if he would feel what
Florence was.   .   .   .   Compared with
modern cities, Florence was but a large
town, and these Pazzi were neighbours
and kinsmen of the Medici, and they and
their fathers had seen the time when the
Medici were no more in the State than
other families which had perhaps scorned
to rise by their arts."

Whatever may have been the virtuous

scruples of the Pazzi and the superior arts
of the Medici, all Florence, and the world
that knew Florence, appreciated the glittering fact of the Medici's eminence.

On the golden afternoon we have chosen
for our visit to the Villa Careggi, where
—to borrow once more from the master of
terse and comprehensive English to whom
we owe *Tuscan Cities*,—" Lorenzo made
a dramatic end twenty years after the
tragedy in the Cathedral,"—we pass sundry statues and mural tablets to Cosimo,
" *Pater Patriæ*," and more Medici coats-of-
arms than we care to count. It is an ugly
escutcheon, to our way of thinking, with
a strong dash of the absurd in the big
boluses jutting out from the surface of the
shield to keep the ages in mind of the
membership in the Guild of the Druggists
or the Apothecaries. The taunt that the
founder of the imperial house made, first,
an honest living, then, a less honest fortune, by compounding and rolling pills,
belongs to a later generation of critics
than the contemporary enemies of the
Medici. They, at least, were acquainted

with the law enacted in 1282, by which
none but the heads of manual arts, trad-
ers, or bankers, were eligible to the principal offices of the State. The *bourgeoisie*
were masters in the city by reason of their
wealth and numbers, and were ungenerous
in the use of their power.

"Members of the aristocratic party
were permitted to enroll themselves in
any guild or art without more than a nominal adoption of the craft in question, by
way of retaining their political rights,"
says a chronicler of those complex times,
and reminds us that "Dante Alighieri,
poeta fiorentino," belonged to the Guild
of the Apothecaries, while his father
was a member of the Wool Merchants'
Guild.

The haughty Medici, in their haughtiest
days, were so far from being ashamed of
their escutcheon, that they stuck shield
and balls—otherwise boluses—upon every
façade and corner where was room or
reason for displaying them. We have
found them in Umbrian, as in Tuscan
cities, and the many that remain must re-

present but a tithe of those that were here in the reign of Il Magnifico.

Before quitting the city for the Villa Careggi, we diverge from the direct route to make a critical study of the Uffizi statue of Lorenzo de' Medici, representing him as he was in the heyday of his puissance. The sculptor would have done his best to flatter his illustrious subject to the extremest verge of compatibility with truthfulness. Yet it would be easier to fancy that we are looking at a caricature than upon a portrait of a patron whose vanity was as patent as his gilded despotism. His grandfather, the great Cosimo, lorded it with a high hand, but he looked the real benevolence he felt for the people calling themselves his children. The cold sneer Grazzini has petrified for us was upon Lorenzo's lip when murder, or rapine, or pleasure was the business of the hour.

" There was something sinister and hateful in his face," if we are to believe Villari.

" The complexion was greenish, the

LORENZO THE MAGNIFICENT.

"There was something sinister and hateful in his face."

mouth very large, the nose flat, and the
voice nasal. *But*"—(even with hypercriti-
cal biographers there must be a "but")—
"But his eye was quick and keen, his forehead was high, and his manner had all of
gentleness that can be imagined of an age
so refined and elegant as that. His conversation was full of vivacity, wit, and
learning. Those who were admitted to
his familiarity were always fascinated by
him."

Mrs. Oliphant's invaluable *Makers of
Florence* thus treats of the magnificent
tyrant :

"Lorenzo reigned in the midst of a
lettered crowd of classic parasites and
flatterers, writing poems which his courtiers found better than Alighieri's, and
surrounding himself with those eloquent
slaves who make a prince's name more
famous than arms or victories, and who
have left a prejudice in the minds of all
literature-loving people in favour of their
patron. A man of superb health and
physical power who can give himself up
to debauch all night without interfering

with his power of working all day, and whose mind is so versatile that he can sack a town one morning and discourse upon the beauties of Plato the next, and weave joyous ballads through both occupations—gives his flatterers reason when they applaud him. . . . The age of Lorenzo was hopeless, morally, full of debauchery, cruelty, and corruption, violating oaths, betraying trusts, believing in nothing but Greek manuscripts, coins, and statues, caring for nothing but pleasure."

An Italian historian supplies the details of the picture of what Lorenzo and his troop of worshippers claimed was the Augustan Age of art-loving Florence:

" Poets of every kind, gentle and simple, with golden cithern and with rustic lute, came from every quarter to animate the suppers of the Magnifico. Whosoever sang of arms, of love, of saints, of fools, was welcome, or he who, drinking, kept the company amused. . . .

" Of all these feasts and masquerades Lorenzo was the inventor and master, his great wealth helping him in his undertak-

ings. In the darkening of twilight it
was his custom to issue forth into the city,
to amuse himself with incredible pomp
and a great retinue on horse and on foot,
more than five hundred in number, with
concerts of musical instruments, singing
in many voices, all sorts of canzones, mad-
rigals, and popular songs. When the night
fell, four hundred servants with lighted
torches followed, and lighted this baccha-
nalian procession."

From the Riccardi Palace, the town
residence of the Medici, through the city
gates to the mansion that was the luxuri-
ous centre of a cluster of seven Medicean
country-seats, streamed the glittering tide
of revelers, each bent upon living up—or
down—to their favourite watchword, " Upon to-morrow none can count," a variation
of the Fool's song of all ages—" Let us
eat and drink, and be merry, for to-morrow we die."

The two-miles-and-a-half of country
road leading to the Villa Careggi is as
beautiful as the fairest dream of earthly
Eden cast into verse by Lorenzo's poets.

Stone walls and terraces are hung and heaped with roses,—Florentine roses,— outnumbering the green leaves among which they blossom.

Upon entering my chamber after breakfast this morning I found it fragrant as a bower in Bendemeer from the deep litter of damp rose-petals scattered upon the carpet to lay the dust before the housemaid swept it, as wet tea-leaves are used in America. After petals and dust are removed together, the delicate aroma lingers in the air for hours.

Whether or not the pretty custom prevailed in Lorenzo's time, he set and followed the like fashion in a wider and more significant sense. He entered voluntarily upon no path that was not soft and sweet with roses. They made rough places smooth to his feet and goodly to look upon ; they laid the dust of popular discontent and enervated the judgment of critics. He stole away the hearts and drugged the consciences of the people by pageants for the present, and promises of greater abundance for days to come, and was in nothing

more consistent than in the brilliant con-
formity of his own life to the Epicurean
philosophy he taught to others :

" Roses to-day, if to-morrow the rue ! "

If he ever bethought himself of a possible hour when roses would die and the
bitter breath of the rue fill his world, he
made no sign of misgiving for all those
twenty years of prosperous pleasures.
White clusters of honey-sweet locust-
blossoms mingle their scent with the breath
of the queen of the flowery kingdom.
Lush grasses carpet the meadows ; vines
and mulberry- and fig-trees are tender
green, and the leaves of olive-orchards
shine in the sun like frosted silver.   The
scarred forehead of Fiesole looks grimly
across the valley down upon her old and
victorious rival, Florence, and Morello
shows, rounded and clear, against a cloud-
less horizon, in serene augury of a fine
morrow.

" *Quando Monte Morello ha il cappello,*
Prendi il mantello."

(When Mt. Morello wears a cap, take a cloak.)

Villa Careggi is well hidden from the public road and eye behind her tall gates and luxuriant plantations of ilex, willows, and beeches. The gardens through which we stroll in a sort of ecstatic trance before entering the house, could not have been more beautiful when Il Magnifico paced the alleys, in grave discussion of the Aristotelian philosophy with a learnèd Greek guest, or chatted of Florence scandals and exchanged gay repartees with his least objectionable favourite, gentle Pico della Mirandola, seated lovingly beside him on one of the arboured stone benches near the fountain-pool, masked, to-day, with lily-pads. A branchy vine covers the wall capped by "the prettily painted loggia, where Lorenzo used to sit with his friends, overlooking Val d'Arno, and glimpsing the Tower of Giotto and the Dome of Brunelleschi." The thousand odours pressed from the wilderness of flowers below by the fall of evening dews, must have regaled their senses while talk and

LILIED POOL AND FOUNTAIN IN GROUNDS OF VILLA CAREGGI.

song went on, and when the wind blew
from the east it would have brought the
sweet clangour of bells from the Campanile,
the Palazzo Vecchio, and a score of minor
towers and steeples.

The room in which Il Magnifico lan-
guished for so many weeks in the spring
of 1492 that we wonder no story has come
to us, as from the Grand Monarque's
death-chamber, of sarcastic apology to his
courtiers for "taking such an unconscion-
able time in dying," overlooks the loveli-
est parterres of the garden.

There is modern furniture here, and we
gravely suspect that the mural decora-
tions commemorative of the glories of the
Medici may have been amplified and "restored" since the eagle eyes were bleared
with the weary gazing upon them. But
the greenery, and the flush of an April
rain of blossoms, the fair pleasure-grounds,
the "tall cypress-bough," and the sheeny
olives outlying the garden-walls, the hazy
domes and turrets of the Florence he had
beautified and corrupted, were what we
see through the casement opposite the

great, sombre bed in which, it is said, he died.

He was but forty-four years old, and for almost thirty of those years he had been his own master, inventing vices when the vulgar routine of familiar excesses was exhausted. His forefathers had had their fill of an evil vintage, and left to him a heritage which, in the course of nature, would have told upon his phenomenal con-stitution without the sapping and mining done of his own accord and at his wild will.

He kept up a merry show, if not a brave heart, during the first month of his illness. Flatterers many, and a few true friends, relieved one another in the task, more difficult each day, of cheating him into forgetfulness of physical agony and of what these were surely, if slowly, bringing toward him.

"The strangest thing of all is, that in all this variety of life they cannot cite a solitary act of real generosity toward his people, his friends, or his kinsmen; for surely if there had been such an act, his indefatigable flatterers would not have forgotten it," Villari says, sardonically.

The assertion throws a lurid glare upon that death-bed, and the emulous group about it. Poets brought new verses for his criticism, and the players upon instruments were there, with professional and paid wits, and knots of nobly born youths, with tales of court amours and quarrels. And, behind them, closing in upon them in their follies, and him in his pain, a cordon of ghastly shapes he alone of them all saw, and even he, dauntless and defiant of other enemies, feared with growing horror. Dread and horror broke forth at last. He was about to die and he would not die unconfessed. But one man would deal honestly with his guilty soul. He bade his attendants send for Savonarola.

In turning back to the life of the Prior of San Marco we read that Giovanni Pico della Mirandola—" a court butterfly, and the most learned creature that ever fluttered near a prince, but of amiable sentiments and tender-heartedness, and the kindly insight of an unspoiled heart "—

had wrought upon Lorenzo, a dozen years
or so before this honest hour, to recall to
Florence and San Marco "the only man
who dared stand, face to face, with himself, and tell him he had done wrong."

Our hearts are drawn out in fond admiration for this "butterfly," and, if only
for the love borne him by Lorenzo, we in-
cline to demur at the pitiless dictum of
Villari. We can, and we do, believe that
the splendid scholar—who lent a reverent
ear and receptive heart to the teachings of
Savonarola, and who, after Lorenzo's
death, would have become a Dominican
monk and entered San Marco had not his
own early decease prevented the fulfillment
of his wish; who, in dying, charged the
Prior of San Marco to see to it that he
was buried in the habit of the order—was,
as historians insist, "a noble young gentleman amid all his frippery of courtier and
virtuoso." He was among the last visitors admitted to this chamber when what
the dying man named as "the last evening
of his winter" (a dreary commentary upon
his dazzling career!) settled darkly about

him.   He had had his final discourse with
his son Piero, of whose disastrous sovereignty the shrewd statesman had more
than a rude premonition.   The conversation was a distress, the farewell was hopeless agony, and the exhausted sufferer
gasped out "a wish to see Pico della Mirandola again, who immediately hastened
to him. . . .

" It appeared as if the sweet expression
of that benevolent and gentle young man
had soothed him a little, for he said to him,
' I should have died unhappy if I had not
first been cheered by a sight of thy face.'"

The beautiful touch of natural human
emotion is the only gleam that falls from
history or tradition across the gloom of
that fateful scene.

We like to think that the gentle impor-
tunity of this best-beloved friend was the
means by which the famous interview with
Savonarola was brought about. The Prior
had not always been amenable to Il Magnifico's blandishments and commands.
When Lorenzo was seen walking, unat-
tended, in the garden of San Marco, the

friars, impressed as by a visit from Jove in person, flew to the Prior's cell to tell him of the honour conferred upon him and their house.

"Has he asked to see me?" asked Savonarola, just raising his head from his desk, and, upon hearing that his magnificent guest had spoken with no one,— "Then leave him to his meditations!"

As if Lorenzo had sought the retreat for no other purpose than to think and to pray.   The gold put into the alms-box by the lord of Florence was carefully set aside from the silver and copper and sent to San Martino for the poor.

"We do not want so much money," was the simple excuse for the apparent ungraciousness of the act, but Lorenzo comprehended that the steadfast preacher was neither to be flattered nor bribed into so much as a passive condoning of his sins as man and ruler.   It was not till Savonarola was assured by a second messenger from Villa Careggi that Il Magnifico was really dying and earnestly desirous to see him, that he made ready to go to him.

He came from San Marco on foot, as
he was wont to travel.   In the black robe
of his order, the cowl drawn over his sad
brows, he crossed the fertile valley we are
looking upon now, and strode up the
gentle eminence where Careggi sat, a
stately planet among her six satellite vil-
las, all belonging to the proud house whose
chief was in the death-throe.   Was it
among the olives down there, or in the
broad, open road bordered by smiling
vineyards, or, maybe, beside the lilied
fountain-pool in the garden, in close view
of this window, that he paused to say to
the lay-brother in attendance upon him,—
" Lorenzo will die " ?   He knew it as well
then as when, the dust of the way white
upon his sandals, he bent his ear to the
confession of the penitent.

Prominent among the " three things that
dragged Lorenzo back and threw him into
despair," and which he doubted if God
would ever pardon, was the murder of as
many of the house of Pazzi as he could
lay his revengeful hands upon after the
assassination of his young brother Giuliano

17

and the attempt upon his own life. The
other two were the brutal pillage of the
town of Volterra, and the robbery of the religious house of Monte delle Fanciulle.

Penitent and confessor were alone in this
stately chamber. Lorenzo was propped
by pillows in the bed, and Savonarola sat,
with bowed head, at his right hand, mur-
muring in the intervals of a recital that
grew in anguish and incoherence with the
rehearsal of each haunting crime,—" God
is good! God is merciful!"

But when the distracted man listened
for the "*absolvo te*" that should follow
these gracious platitudes, the deep voice
of the Prior thrilled through the stillness
upon the dulling ear as his Master's may
have smote that of the young ruler, and
in somewhat the same words:

"Three things are required of you."

We will let Villari tell the rest:

"'And what are they, Father?' replied
Lorenzo.

"Savonarola's countenance became
grave, and, raising the fingers of his right
hand, he thus began:

"'First,—it is necessary that you

should have a full and lively faith in the mercy of GOD.'

" ' That I have, most fully.'

" ' Secondly, it is necessary to restore that which you unjustly took away, or enjoin your sons to restore it for you.'

" This requirement appeared to cause him surprise and grief. However, with an effort, he gave his consent by a nod of his head.

" Savonarola then rose up, and while the dying prince shrank with terror upon his bed, the confessor seemed to rise above himself when saying :

" ' *Lastly,—you must restore liberty to the people of Florence !* '

" His countenance was solemn, his voice almost terrible, his eyes, as if to read the answer, remained fixed intently on those of Lorenzo, who, collecting all the strength that nature had left him, turned his back on him, and scornfully, without uttering a word.

" And thus Savonarola left him, without giving him absolution ; and the Magnificent, lacerated by remorse, soon after breathed his last."

XIV

AS IN DAVID'S DAY

XIV

AS IN DAVID'S DAY

WE had talked of nothing at dinner but the invitation received and accepted that day.

"I have arranged for your good pleasure 'A Syrian Evening,'" said the quaintly pretty note of the Syrian-born hostess. "We hope to see you and your friends at nine o'clock to-night."

At last our dreams of the poetry of motion, as expressed by the Oriental dancer, and the rich imagery of Oriental improvisation, were to be fulfilled. We let our imaginations revel, unchecked, in our table-talk of Miriam tossing her timbrel aloft, leading the women who went after her with timbrels, and the triumphant chant that arose above the ground-swell of the Red Sea. Of Jephthah's

daughter, ringing and tinkling a welcome
to the victorious chief.   How, as far back
as the days of Job, the tabret was in use,
and men rejoiced with the timbrel and
harp.   A pocket Webster instructed us as
to the identity of the tabret with the tabor
of later times, and that both meant a
small drum.

Our antiquarian prosed learnedly upon
what he called " Nebuchadnezzar's wind-
and-string band," enlightening us as to the
forms and uses of the ancient cornet, flute,
harp, sackbut, psaltery, and dulcimer, until
affronted by the amateurish attempt of a
mischief-loving youth to establish a near
relationship between sackbut and bagpipe.
Whereat the man of science waxed wroth
and dumb.

It was, then, an expectant and gleeful
party that packed itself into three carriages
and left the walled city by the Jaffa gate,
turning quickly to the right and into a
maze of muddy lanes, lined on both sides
with stone walls topped with bunches of
dried thorn-bushes, laid in mortar, after
the manner of the broken-bottle *chevaux*

de frise of more enlightened lands. A
moonlight drive of half a mile brought us
to the gate of a garden surrounding one of
the square stone houses that are springing
up rapidly in the suburbs of Jerusalem.
Our host met us at the gate, and led us
through the porch into a big hall which
took up half of the ground-floor of the
dwelling. We had but a hasty view of a
lighted room packed with "people making
a noise," as we were hurried across one
corner of this hall and into an inner apartment, neatly furnished in European style
as a parlour.   There we were seated close
to the open door of communication with
the larger room. All the light in the
parlour came through this door, and we
now perceived that the men of our company were theoretically invisible, or, at
best, represented to the revellers by their
astral bodies.

The merry-makers were all women, and
a certain fine unconsciousness of the existence of the foreign spectators was inimitable and impressive. Not an eye
wandered in our direction, although two

foreign consuls, whom most of the assembly must have known by sight, were with us, and a young English traveller, as brawny as Hercules and handsome as Apollo, leaned against the door-frame just where the light from the outer room threw his profile into bold relief upon the dark background.

The noise, unabated by our intrusion, went on steadily when we were seated and could define and classify the hubbub. The performers, and a few old women with babies in their laps, sat flat upon the matted floor, their feet tucked under them. All were in gala dress—jewelry gleaming upon arms, hair, and hands. The married women wore the picturesque *mendel*. This is a square of thin, flowered—embroidered or plain—coloured muslin, edged with silk lace. When the wearer is indoors, one-half of the *mendel* is folded back, kerchief-wise, upon the top of her head. When she goes abroad, she pulls this over her face, making a triangular veil through which she can see, but which masks her features.

Each of the younger women had a
musical instrument of some sort.   A miniature drum,—which we took to be the
"tabor" or "tabret,"—set on the floor in
front of her and beaten with the knuckles,
was the most popular.   There were also
tambourines (timbrels?) and cymbals, and
something, not unlike a mandolin in shape,
with short, taut strings that twanged as
shrilly as cicadæ, above the shallow roll of
drum and tambourine.

"I think," said the Mischief-lover,
meditatively, with a demure glance at the
Antiquarian, "I—am—quite—sure—that
those are sackbuts! Or, maybe, dulci-
mers."

There was no time in the "music."
Our ears presently discerned rhythm; a
wave-like vibration in the drumming, hum-
ming, and shrilling, that doubtless represented time to the initiated. After
the hostess had made us welcome, she
took her stand in a cleared space in the
middle of the hall.   Holding a tambourine,
and shaking it as she moved, with now and
then a touch of a deft thumb to the tight

"head," she began to dance, very slowly and gracefully, advancing a few steps and receding as many, smiling and beckoning to one and another of the cross-legged figures. She kept this up for several minutes before a plump, black-eyed little body arose from a corner and obeyed the mute invitation. She was dressed in a bright blue silk gown, unpicturesquely Parisian in cut and fit. The Oriental element was supplied by the blue *mendel*, and by ropes of gold chains dangling below her girdle, which was also of gold, and flexible like the fine meshes of a coat of mail.

Taking the tambourine from the other's hand, she went through the same *pas seul;* five or six steps forward, as many backward, varied by swayings of the body above the waist-line, whirling the tambourine about her head, and shaking it to the right and left. The steps were a shuffle, her feet never leaving the floor. While she danced, the " rubadub " of tabrets and tambourines, the twanging of the mandolins, and the measured clapping of hands

("For all the world like 'Pease porridge hot,'" said the Mischief-lover in my ear) went on with increasing fervour.

"Sometimes they are really intoxicated by the music," said a consul's wife, who had lived in Jerusalem ten years. "I have felt the exhilaration myself upon several occasions. There is something in the rhythmic beat that gets into the blood and the head."

It did not get into ours. Indeed, the noise was becoming tiresome and the spectacle monotonous when—after a succession of eight or ten women had had the floor, each repeating her predecessor's motions—the hostess again appeared, and clapped her hands sharply three times. Servants answered the signal, and passed, first to us, then to the performers, trays containing tiny cups of black coffee, glasses of native wine, and wedges of layer-cake, filled with dead-sweet conserves that made the wine taste as sour as vinegar.

While the refreshments were going around, a woman's voice was raised from the back of the hall. She was young and rather comely, and her scarlet skirt did not quite hide a pair of trim feet encased in white silk stockings and red slippers. Raising her tabret to the level of her forehead, and dealing it a smart thump to attract attention, she uttered in a high monotone a string of rapid Arabic, getting in, I should say, fifty words between every two breaths, and winding up all with a screeched "*a-a-a-h-h !*" of which written words can give no adequate idea.

Our dragoman interpreted the outburst. It was a florid panegyric upon our host, his many virtues, personal gifts, and worthy deeds, and the expression of a hope that he and his posterity would live forever.

A second breathless and headlong recitation from another woman did the decent and dutiful thing by the hostess, who, being in sight, waved and kissed her hand in acknowledgment. Other personages whom the company delighted to honour were dry-toasted in due order. Each improvisation ended with the unwritable, ear-piercing "*a-a-a-h-h !*" always running up the scale in precisely the same key and

ending abruptly upon the highest note of
the gamut.

The hostess brought forward next a
new and striking figure.

"A distinguished professional," commented the interpreter.   " She has been
married twice, both times to white men,
who were won by her remarkable talents."

Her good looks had no share in the con-
quest.   She was a Nubian—full-blooded,
as was proved by her coal-black skin and
woolly hair—broad of shoulder, and long
of limb.   Her gown of dark blue cloth was
girdled loosely with a crimson sash, and
fell in easy folds to her feet.   She looked
like what was called in *ante-bellum* par-
lance, "a field-hand."   From every side
of the great hall arose a wild clamour of
beaten drums, and clanging cymbals,
shaken tambourines, and clapping hands,
an accompaniment that was not inter-
mitted through what followed.   The Nubian smiled widely upon her admirers,
squatted upon the mat, and began to bat-
ter a small drum furiously, rocking from
side to side, then back and forth, rolling

up her eyes, and showing a double row of white teeth in a grimace of cumulative ecstasy. Bounding suddenly to her full height by one surprising effort of her supple body, not touching the floor with her hands, she entered upon a series of spiral exercises, keeping her feet perfectly still as a pivotal centre, and swinging outward from them. The tabret was pounded madly all the time.

This dizzying exhibition ended, she drew a white handkerchief from her bosom, wrapped it about her left arm, and went through the motions of dandling and hushing a child to sleep, crooning a fantastic, tuneless lullaby, and shuffling her feet in time with it. Waking the baby with a genuine negro " ki-yi ! " and shaking the handkerchief into the air, she danced to a more lively measure, throwing herself forward, then backward, farther and farther each time, until a topple and fall seemed inevitable. In one of the forward inclinations she dexterously spread her handkerchief upon the floor, and in another picked it up with her teeth, a feat

A SYRIAN PROFESSIONAL DANCER AND MUSICIAN.
From photograph in *Christian Herald* Collection.

that elicited deafening applause. A final figure of the so-called dance bore some resemblance, as I was told afterwards, to the objectionable *danse de ventre.* In comfortable ignorance of the circumstance we looked on, unmoved and unsympathetic, while the assembly, lined up three deep against the walls of the central hall, vented their delight in louder and faster drummings and clapping of hands.

A laugh, smothered by politeness as soon as it was born, rippled through the group of unseen lookers-on as the handsome Hercules in the doorway turned to say, *sotto voce,* but energetically, while the Nubian was in the thick of her triumphs :

" By Jove ! what a fool King Herod must have been ! "

Before twelve o'clock, set by us as the hour of departure, curiosity had given place to ennui, and ennui deepened into boredom of a pronounced type. We were glad to make our exit with the same pretence of stealth that had attended our entrance. The cool, delicious dampness of a Syrian winter night that met us with-

18

out made us comprehend what the atmosphere had been within.   The consul's
wife told us, on the way home, that the
scene we were leaving behind us represented all that the Syrian woman ever
knows of a "revel."   She never speaks to
a man until she is married, unless he be
her near kinsman.   After marriage, even
stricter laws govern her association with
the other sex.   They have no dancing, or
conversation, or dinner-parties where men
and women meet on equal and pleasant
social terms ; no libraries and no clubs
where women can acquire knowledge and
exchange views upon higher topics than
the details of their dull, eventless lives.
The fifty-odd women we had left sitting
cross-legged on the matting, their backs
against the wall, their tabrets on the floor
in front of them, just as we had found
them three hours before, would talk of
this evening of dissipation for weeks to
come.

The Mischief-lover's face was sombre
in the moonlight ; his tone was regretful.

"The evening has been full of disillu-

sions," he lamented.   " And I 'm afraid, if
the truth could be known, we should learn
that the women who came out, singing
and dancing, to meet King Saul with tabrets and other instruments, and answered
one another as they played, rattled off,—
' Saul-hath-slain-his-thousands-and-David-
his-ten-thousands-*a-a-h-h* !' just as those
girls ' said their pieces.' The East is a
changeless land, you know—more's the
pity !"

At noon on the morrow we sent a note
of thanks to our hostess. The messenger
brought back word that she was not yet
out of bed. The fun (?) had raged on
until *nine o'clock* A.M., and the gracious
mistress of ceremonies was " somewhat
fatigued."

XV

IN VILLETTE

XV

IN VILLETTE

"THE building in the Rue d'Isabelle
will shortly be pulled down."

"The many admirers of Charlotte
Brontë will regret to learn that the Pensionnat Héger, made famous by her novel
Villette, has been demolished to make
way for a row of modern houses."

Both of these items were read by us on
the steamer which brought us from America, four months ago. As newspaper
paragraphs go, they should have had
weight in directing the trend of our roam-
ings on this, our first day in Brussels.
Had our faith in them been positive it is
doubtful if we should have come to the
miniature Paris. Waterloo was not an
irresistible attraction, nor did the lace
warehouses turn the scales of our unfriv-

olous mood. We are here because Brussels is " Villette," and an impulse we are ready, in the end, to respect as inspiration, moved us to see, with bodily vision, a locality familiar to the mind's eye, to wit, Madame Beck's " Pensionnat de Demoiselles," in the " Rue Fossette."

We called it by the every-day name of Rue d'Isabelle in consulting the feminine Autocrat of our *pension* déjeuner-table, a suave Presence of boundless information and limited English vocabulary. She took refuge in Brussels-French in the desire to be fluent, yet explicit. She had heard of Charlotte Brontë's historical (!) novel, and that the scene was laid in the respectable and eminent Pensionnat of Monsieur and Madame Héger. In passing, she might be permitted to say that the Pensionnat was in the Avenue Louise, not in the Rue d'Isabelle. The trifling mistake was quite pardonable in Mesdames. Both were the names of women. Madame Héger died in 1889, and it is now three years since the lamented demise of Monsieur Héger at the great age of eighty-seven.

Mademoiselle, their accomplished daughter, still conducts the school for young
ladies in the Avenue Louise. If Mesdames would have the goodness to look
from the window of the salon, she—the
Autocrat—would take pleasure in indicat-
ing the very handsome house.

It is a handsome house, large, square,
white, with a plentiful complement of
windows, a very model of monumental
and prosperous respectability, and we
forthwith disbelieved in it with all our
might.   The situation upon the corner of
a spick-and-span Boulevard gave the lie
direct to our preconceptions of the sombre age of Madame Beck's Pensionnat.
When inquiries of neighbouring shopkeepers extracted the admission that there
was not, and never had been, a Rue d'Isabelle within two miles of Avenue Louise,
we should have given up the quest in despair, but for a conviction that would
not down at talk of demolition and over-
turning and recasting of streets and
houses.   In the persuasion, as irrational
as it was obstinate, that we knew Brussels

as Villette better than our well-informed landlady, we repudiated her pilotage and trusted ourselves recklessly to the chart furnished by Charlotte herself.

Lucy Snowe had followed Dr. John— then a stranger who spoke English and offered to guide her to her inn—"through the double gloom of trees and fog," across a park, and, losing her bearings after he left her, strayed to a flight of steps, which she descended. "In a very quiet and comparatively clean and well-paved street," was the Pensionnat.

Our first step was to find the Park. It was half-an-hour's drive from the square white house on the spick-and-span Boulevard. Let me say here, in justice to the Autocrat, that the building in question, as transpired subsequently, really is the Pensionnat Héger and is presided over by Madame Beck's daughters. If we had sought information there touching the *ci-devant* pupil-teacher of their lady-mother's reign, would we have met Fifine and Désirée? Madame refused to see Mrs. Gaskell when she would have "in-

terviewed " her on the subject of Charlotte's residence in her school, *Villette*, in
spite of the author's emphatic interdiction,
having been translated into French by
that time, and read by Madame and her
circle. The probability that the aversion
to the Brontës and all that pertained to
them is hereditary, forbade the thought
of application to the Demoiselles Héger
in our dilemma.

The Park is bright and dry to-day, yet
a subtle sense of familiarity with trees
and walks besets us as we enter it. The
belief that we are following John Bretton's
" frank tread " and Lucy's soundless footsteps, takes fast hold of us. Without at-
tempting to analyse the sensation, we
quicken our pace and are led straight to
the top of a flight of stone steps, with a
drop of, perhaps, a dozen feet, into a quiet
street, and at the bottom a long block of
houses which we immediately identify as
the " Pensionnat de Demoiselles."

Fin-de-siècle scepticism halts us even
here. Instead of going straight to our
work, we turn weakly aside into the Eng-

lish Bank close to the short stairway, and
have the grace to blush at the uninten-
tional rebuke of our lack of faith in our
"inward leading," conveyed in the civil
reply to our inquiries.

"You have only to go down those steps
and you are there ! The house is now occupied by a public school. Pulled down !
Bless me ! nothing of the sort ! It stands
just where it did, and *as* it did, fifty years
ago."

By the means truthfully recorded here,
we have arrived at our goal. *Villette* and
Lucy Snowe are more trustworthy *ciceroni*
than Brussels-bred Autocrat and shopkeepers.

Our ring at the door is answered by a
black-eyed sub-teacher, whose position is
precisely what Charlotte's was during her
second term at the Pensionnat Héger,
after she had returned without Emily, and
alone. The guide is polite and willing,
and, as we have chanced to call upon a
festa holiday, is cordially at our service.
As she does not speak English, she has
never read *Villette*, she says, and we re-

PUBLIC PARK OF BRUSSELS.

frain from allusion to the obnoxious French
edition.

"But I know the book quite well," she
continues. "So many English and Americans—many more Americans than English—come here every year, and talk, oh,
so much! of Mademoiselle Lucie and
Madame Beck and Mademoiselle Charlotte, and the Ghost"— laughing brightly
—"that I seem to myself to have read of
them all."

In forecasting this visit, our minds were
taken up by thoughts of the two Yorkshire
girls, abruptly transplanted to the foreign
pensionnat, as out-of-place, and as ill-at-
ease as would be two larks snared upon
the Haworth moors and kept in a Belgian
cage. We lost Charlotte and Emily as
soon as we struck upon Dr. Bretton's track,
and felt the presence of the pale mute
shadow that "would have followed that
frank tread through continual night, to
the world's end."

I have always maintained that Lucy
was more truly in love with this "true
young English gentleman," with his

"beamy head," "bonny wells of eyes, arch mouth, and gay smile," than with the "dark little man, pungent and austere," who, even to her would-be partial eyes, "seemed a harsh apparition, with his close-shorn black head, broad, sallow brow, thin cheek, wide and quivering nostril." Affection for the one was a glad, spontaneous upspringing; for the other, a matter of painstaking cultivation. Long after she believed that she had found her soul-counterpart in the acerb Professor, the confession escapes her in meditating upon what she had denied to her trusting heart :

"Was this feeling dead? I do not know, but it was buried. Sometimes I thought the tomb unquiet and dreamed strangely of disturbed earth, and of hair still golden and living, obtruded through coffin chinks."

The man she loved and the man who loved her, keep step with us in our passage through the corridors and the class-rooms where Lucy gave English lessons, and conquered the mutinous "titled belles in the first row who had sat down predetermined that a *bonne d'enfants* should

not be set over them," and locked up
Catalonian Dolores in the book-closet,
still to be seen. Bare, clean, and comfortless as is the suite, it was yet drearier before the larger rooms were divided by
partitions for the convenience of the present occupants. The long *classe*, cold at
early morning and at night, "with the
nipping severity of a Continental winter,"
which Lucy paced fast to keep herself
warm when the "popish *lecture pieuse* from
that guilty old book containing legends of
the saints, was brought out in the only
warm place in the house, the refectory—
the scene of the *Etude du soir*"—has
been cut up into three compartments. It
was her chosen haunt when she was off
duty, her promenade, her study, her oratory, her resort, when physical exercise
and solitude were absolute needs to the
overwrought spirit. She was "fortu-
nate if the moon shone, and, if there
were stars, soon reconciled to their dim
gleam, or even to the total eclipse of
their absence."

At least we can look out of the windows

through which their light crossed her lonely beat. In the refectory we provoke the curiosity of our little companion by setting the stage for the ridiculous exhibition of "the wicked, venomous little man's" temper, on the evening when " Mees Lucie" "swept away her working materials to clear space for his book, and withdrew herself to make room for his person," and, "flint and tinder that he was! he struck and took fire directly."

How well we know it all! and how present and vivid is the reproduction here in the marble-paved room, looking out upon the garden which we are reserving for the last and choicest *morceau* of the continual feast!

Before tasting this we mount to the dormitories. Our vivacious conductor is eager to show us where, in the now empty room,—all the pupils in the public school being "*externes*,"—Charlotte and Emily Brontë's beds used to stand. In consideration of the "reserved habits of the English," they were allowed to draw a curtain between that extremity of the large apartment and the twenty beds that filled the remaining space.

We refuse to see anybody but Lucy Snowe, lonely and wakeful, while "stretched on the nineteen beds lay nineteen forms at full length, and motionless"; Lucy, battling, in the desperation of a drowning wretch, with grim Reason, who bade her put at once out of her mind, and finally, the vision of golden-haired John Bretton, "good and sweet, but not for her," and revel no more in the "strange, sweet insanity," luring her to forgetfulness of the truth that she "was born only to work for a piece of bread; to await the pains of death, and steadily, through all life, to despond." To the dormitory she stole with Dr. John's first letter in her hand, "in haste and trembling lest Madame should creep up-stairs and spy her," and "folding the treasure, yet all fair and inviolate, in silver paper, put it into a casket and the casket into a drawer of the bureau" (we designate the very corner then filled by the bureau), "shut up box and drawer, reclosed, re-

locked the dormitory, and descended to
classe, feeling as if fairy-tales were true,
and fairy gifts no dream."

The dormitory, where we select her
"own casement" out of which she "leaned
on summer evenings, as ever solitary, to
look out upon the gay little city, and hear
the band play in the park, thinking mean-
time my own thoughts, living my own life
in my own still shadow-world."

We open the casement to see the ledge
on which she sat through the thunder-
storm that awoke all the sleepers in the
dormitory. While the rest knelt around
the night-lamp, praying aloud, she remained without, upon her perch, her feet
upon the roof of a lower adjoining building.

"It was wet, it was wild, it was pitch-
dark. I could not go in. Too resistless
was the delight of staying with the wild
hour, black, and full of thunder, pealing
out such an ode as language never deliv-
ered to man."

"The attic was no pleasant place," we
quote in English on entering what is

THE GARRET IN MADAME BECK'S HOUSE.

gained by another flight of stairs. "In summer weather it was hot as Africa, in winter it was always cold as Greenland. Well was it known to be tenanted by rats, by black beetles and by cockroaches— nay, rumour affirmed that the ghostly Nun of the garden had once been seen there."

The sub-teacher's laugh is as ready as light. She has caught the sense of the last words. Tripping over the dusty, echoing floor, she points to a small window or glazed trap-door in the sloping roof, dim and cobwebby, for the attic is disused now, even as a lumber room :

"*Par là !*" she says, and we see that the trick of the pseudo ghost is known to her.

Lucy did not believe in the Nun when she "opened the skylight, dragged a large, empty chest beneath it, and, having mounted upon a smaller box, ascended this species of extempore throne," and began the study of the part forced upon her by the remorseless Professor. But she saw the apparition on the winter night when she sought the " deep, black, cold garret," to read, in the solitude she could get nowhere else, the letter she had locked away at noon, the seal unbroken.

" That present moment had no pain, no blot, no want.   Full, pure, perfect, it deeply blessed me. . . .   Dr. John ! you pained me afterwards.   Forgiven be every ill—freely forgiven—for the sake of that one dear, remembered good."

Then, a movement in the obscure recess behind her, and—" I saw in the middle of that ghostly chamber a figure all black or white ; the skirts straight, narrow, black ; the head bandaged, veiled, white."

Lucy ! still, Lucy ! and nowhere are her being and her presence a more vital actuality than in the garden behind the low pile of school buildings.   The grounds of the Pensionnat are no longer spacious. At least one-half of the original garden has been cut off and built up with new houses.   The forbidden walk (*l'allée défendue*) remains in part, although Methuselah, the ancient pear-tree—" dead " in Lucy's and Charlotte's time, " all but a

FORBIDDEN WALK IN MADAME BECK'S GARDEN, WITH ADJACENT COLLEGE BUILDINGS.

few boughs, which still faithfully renewed
their perfumed snow in spring, and their
honey-sweet pendants in autumn "—perished down to the root long ago. The
large *berceau*, or arbour, shaded by the
acacia, is gone, but the trellised walk
skirting the high, grey wall, "where jasmine and ivy met and were married," is
the same in which Charlotte and Emily
took their silent "constitutional" in all
weathers. Here Lucy encountered Madame Beck in her nightly round of
surveillance, after the casket and note
had fallen "from the window high in the
wall of the adjacent college buildings"
(we look up at the identical casement),
and Dr. John, having seen it dropped,
came to hunt for it and to save Ginevra
Fanshawe from disgrace.

Villette is not fiction, as far as the setting of the story is concerned. Every
feature of house and environs is drawn
with the fidelity of a photograph, taken
by an artist and developed by an adept.
That Madame Beck, M. Paul Emmanuel,
and Ginevra Fanshawe were painted from,

and to, the life, we are informed by Charlotte's schoolfellows and others who knew
the unconscious sitters.   Does this account for the spell that has brought us to
the spot and makes us live out the wonderful tale now that we are here ?

The book is a unique.   For actors, we
have the teachers and pupils of the most
conventional of conventional and Continental boarding-schools.   In a confidential home-letter, Charlotte writes of these,
her associates :

" Amongst 120 persons which compose
the daily population of this house, I can
discern only one or two who deserve anything like regard.   They have not intellect or politeness, or good nature, or
good feeling.   They are nothing.   They
have no sensations themselves, and they
excite none.   .   .   .   *The phlegm that
thickens their blood is too gluey to boil.*"

For theatre, *Villette* had the four walls
of the Pensionnat, and this walled-in garden.   We have, it is true, infrequent
glimpses of streets in the old parts of the
then small city of Brussels, of La Ter-

rasse, the Bretton country-house, and the
salon of the de Bassompierres in the Hotel
Crécy, but the action centres in this dull
house and in the grounds—"a trite, down-
trodden place in the broad, vulgar middle
of the day,"—and at all seasons tamely uninteresting to all but Lucy Snowe, and to
the genius that conceived and brought her
forth. *Villette* was written some years after
Charlotte's connection with the school,
as pupil and as teacher, ceased.   It is not
possible for one who has read the book to
visit Pensionnat and garden without com-
prehending that it "came" to her here.

After Emily went back to Yorkshire,
never to return to the hated school-life,
her sister seemed, to the few who cared to
notice her, utterly alone, her evening strolls
in the "forbidden walk," the twilight rev-
eries upon the rustic seat at the far end of
"the strait and narrow path,"—the bench
she had "reclaimed from mould and fungi,"
—melancholy and purposeless enough to
sink the foreign girl into the slough of
imbecility, or to drive her mad.   Between
her and these alternative fates stood Lucy

and her story, with all that entered into the growth thereof.

"In catalepsy and a dead trance I studiously held the quick of my nature," are words she put into Lucy's mouth.

The quick of Charlotte's nature was instinct with potent germs of thought. At eventide, and in the noon and holiday lingerings in the sequestered alley, shunned by other teachers, and prohibited to the scholars because of the college boarding-houses flanking it—the still air took life; at the lifting of the wand she alone knew that she carried, and even she did not value aright, the dusky solitude was peopled with those who left no room for regret at the loss of visible companionship. She tells it all to us in pages that sparkle with humour and beautiful fancies, and glow with passion.

Legends more than half forgotten, even in Brussels, connect the sunken square about the Pensionnat Héger with tournaments and knightly vows and mediæval romances of various complexions.

"There was a tradition that Madame

IN MADAME BECK'S GARDEN.

"The trellised walk skirting the high grey wall."

Beck's house had, in old days, been a convent. That, in years gone by—before the city had overspread this quarter, and when it was tilled ground and avenue, and such deep and leafy seclusion as ought to embosom a religious house—Something had happened on this site, which, arousing fear and inflicting horror, had left to the place the inheritance of a Ghost Story."

The trivial circumstance that, fifty-seven years ago, a country parson's daughter, plain, provincial in dress and carriage, and already in her thirtieth year, studied, worked, and suffered in this ugly range of houses, and dreamed her own dreams in the old garden, now chill with the shadow of encroaching walls, makes all that went before her residence here like a rubbed pencil-sketch set beside a canvas eloquent with the imagery of genius, transcribed by a master magician's hand.

THE END